The Sava

THE SAVAGE NIGHT

Mohammed Dib

La Nuit sauvage
Translated and with an
introduction
by C. DICKSON

University of Nebraska Press
Lincoln and London

Publication of this translation was assisted by
grants from the National Endowment for the Arts
and the French Ministry of Culture.

Library of Congress Cataloging-in-Publication Data
Dib, Mohammed, 1920-
[Nuit sauvage. English]
The savage night / Mohammed Dib ; translated
and with an introduction by C. Dickson.
p. cm.
ISBN 0-8032-1713-7 (cloth : alk. paper) –
ISBN 0-8032-6620-0 (pbk. : alk. paper)
I. Dickson, C. II. Title
PQ3989.D52 N8513 2001 843'.914–dc21
00-059965

Contents

Translator's Introduction

Mohammed Dib, the prolific Algerian-born writer, is hailed not only as one of the founding fathers of North African literature but more generally as one of the leading French-language authors writing today. Dib suggests that the secret to understanding the diversity of his work lies, paradoxically, at the heart of its discontinuity, in discovering the similarities that contribute to creating a unified whole. In the afterword to this collection, Dib explains that one element unifying his work is the inexplicability of human brutality.

Exiled from his homeland in 1959, Dib has never shied from what he considers the moral responsibility of his role as a writer. Ever faithful to his origins, Dib's roots sink deep into his native land in an attempt to understand those more profound ramifications that are common to the whole of humanity, thereby developing an extraordinary palette of rich and varied themes. This quest lends a distinguished temper to his vision, gives a resonant tone to his voice. He remarks, "The fact that writing entails a risk restores a certain stamp of nobility to literature. Yet today, it is less a question of nobility than one of simple survival in the vast and chattering desert that has spread over a large part of the planet."

Today, more than ever, faced with the untold and ongoing wrongs of our time, Dib's voice rings out in clear protest. The universal struggle for survival that is so often thwarted by the absurdity of the "chatter" — or to be more direct, barbarity — is precisely what many of the tales in The Savage Night bring to light.

The stories in themselves represent a remarkably wide range of points of view and serve as an admirable vehicle for Dib's skilled use of French. Here, the sustained level of language illustrates Dib's uncanny ability to capture a starkly pure reality cleansed of superficiality. As we are led through the astonishing landscape of his imagination, the author's eloquent narratives teeter on that mythical frontier between prose and poetry. His dexterous use of the play of light and shadow throws into sharp contrast the gentle, luminous side of humanity and the savage darkness that lurks in us all.

Before examining the short stories translated in this volume, we should follow Dib's own advice and take the time to put this noteworthy author into the context of his life experience and the body of work he has produced. While the prolific nature of Dib's work makes it impractical to mention each piece (nearly thirty at present) in this overview, it is worthwhile to note that, in addition to fiction, Dib has published several volumes of poetry and is also the author of plays. *Tlemcen ou les lieux de l'écriture* (1995) demonstrates his talent as a photographer as well.

Mohammed Dib was born in Tlemcen, in the west of Algeria, on 21 July 1920. As a child, Dib expressed an early interest in the written word, and he recalls practicing at writing and painting seated in the "posture of a scribe" at the *meïda* (a low table at which the family generally took their meals). He attended primary school, high school, and the first years of university in Tlemcen then completed his studies in the city of Oujda near the eastern border of Morocco. Before becoming a journalist, Dib worked at various jobs — he was a schoolmaster for one year, a French-English interpreter from 1943 to 1944, and manager of a carpet factory in Tlemcen for a few years, where he himself created designs for the carpets.

After having traveled to France for the first time in 1952, Dib published *La Grande Maison*, the first volume of a trilogy that heralded the author's subtle insight and talent as a storyteller. The first novel relates a child's coming of age under French colonialism, in a house shared by several families. Although its tone reflects a penchant for naturalism, *La Grande Maison* does not yet reveal the militancy Dib later espoused. The two books that followed, *L'Incendie* (1954) and *Le Métier à tisser* (1957), are more combative in nature, although telling a good story (which Dib does with consummate skill) remains their primary objective throughout.

Between 1954, which marked the beginning of the Algerian War of Independence, and 1959, when he was expelled from Algeria by colonial authorities for his political activism, Dib published a fourth novel, *Un été africain*, and a collection of short stories, *Au café*. Along with the first trilogy, these works won him not only critical acclaim in his native Maghreb and in France but also the esteem of the literati internationally.

Taking up residence as an expatriate in France in 1959, Dib continued to break ground as an author whose fictional experiments set him apart from the "guerilla linguistics" and revolutionary romanticism that were in vogue among his contemporaries. Dib turned a deaf ear to these trends, never sacrificing the elegance of his language to orchestrate the type of confrontation so common in the popular forms of social realism of the day. His second trilogy — *La Danse du Roi* (1968), *Dieu en Barbarie* (1970), and *Le Maître de chasse* (1973) — was published during this period. Although Algeria is still very present in this work, Dib observes his native land and the devastation of the war for independence from afar. As a result of this distance, the questions posed in these three novels take on a profound and universal quality.

After a period of silence, Dib published what has been qualified as his Nordic trilogy — *Les terrasses d'Orsol* (1985), *Le sommeil d'Eve* (1989), and *Neiges de marbre* (1990). Set in Finland, where he has traveled and spent extended periods of time, the work seems to reflect a voluntary effort to free himself from themes typical to North African literature. Herein Dib meditates on the meaning of exile, expressing oneself in a foreign language, loss of one's identity, and the meeting of two cultures. In all three novels, a man from the South encounters and falls in love with a woman from the North. The succinct story entitled "Talilo is Dead" in *The Savage Night* could be considered an epilogue to *Les terrasses d'Orsol*, as it takes up the same characters and informs us as to what their lives have become.

The theme of exile and the meeting of cultures as symbolized by a mixed couple is also at the heart of Dib's highly acclaimed *L'infante*

Maure, published in 1994. The narrator of the novel, Lyyli Belle, the daughter of just such a couple, confides her innermost thoughts in a magnificent style that wheels and dances with extraordinary poetic freshness. "The Little Girl in the Trees," a story in this collection, captures the undercurrent of this masterful novel. The story is a compact, crystalline gem, condensing the essence of one of this author's major works.

At the end of 1994, Dib was awarded Le Grand Prix de la Francophonie (the highest distinction attributed by the prestigious Académie Française) for the whole of his work. The prize was established for "a writer who has contributed in an eminent fashion to promoting the French language," and Dib was the first person of North African descent to have received this honor. Over the course of his long career, Dib had relentlessly pursued his own quiet, yet heretofore unexplored path far from the fray of angry young men or martyred writers.

The collection of thirteen short stories entitled *The Savage Night*, translated in this volume, appeared in France in the spring of 1995. It is evident from this work that Dib takes his duty as an Algerian writer and spokesman of his day very seriously. Though the collection is inspired by the horror of the current Algerian tragedy, Dib does not limit the thematic development to a specific geographical region. Rather, using his personal experience as a springboard, the violence depicted in the collection is not simply Dib's way of expressing his revolt but also of doing the only thing he believes might possibly be effective. For, as he states in the afterword, to attempt to answer the *why* of the question of human brutality might be asking too much, but "the least we can do is state the *how*, expose human beings for the insidious buffoons they are."

Whether set in present-day Algeria ("The Eye of the Hunter," "The Detour," "A Game of Dice"), depicting the war for independence ("The Savage Night"), or evoking memories of the colonial era ("Amria and the Frenchman," "Life Today"), Dib paints a vivid picture of the diverse facets of the Algerian question. Then suddenly and without warning the author whisks us off to a poverty-stricken village somewhere in Latin America ("Paquita") and to war-torn Sarajevo ("Butterflies").

Slowly, inexorably, Dib unfolds the thirteen tales of this collection as if it were some sort of talisman, to ward off the curse of "the insidious farces of this insidious time," as if he wished to draw back a veil and show us that the senseless violence is a daily reality for many, despite our shameful indifference. Then, perhaps to bring the point closer to home, in "The Merry Misfit" we read of the desperate plight of a man who joins the ranks of the homeless in Paris. Still set in Paris, the ironic tale "Exodus" chronicles the everyday, obtuse bigotry that governs so much of the human race. Then too, somewhere in France, the story entitled "Letter to Mother" relates the violence of madness, brought on by the unbearable, inherited memory of the Holocaust, into which a Jewish youth irrevocably sinks.

It would certainly be a grave oversight to say that *The Savage Night* is filled only with darkness. Even in its most somber moments, redeeming glimmers of light come to the surface — in the poetry of the prose or some gleeful, ironic twist. This contrast is perhaps most marked in the title story as the bright star, which represents the impossible love between the two protagonists, is engulfed in the hellish blast of revolt and hate. In "Talilo is Dead" it is Aïd who, retreating from the world into his own lyrical meditation, lights a beautiful but distant torch that seems to blaze in its wisdom just outside of our reach. At other times the night suddenly lights up, and for an instant, through a child's wonder-struck eyes, the world seems to regain its lost innocence, as in "The Little Girl in the Trees." Dib's child protagonists, whether they are from Algeria, Bosnia, or Latin America, act as ever-present sentinels. They are bearers of light, seekers of truth, perhaps bringing the hope of new tomorrows in a more human world.

C. DICKSON

The Savage Night

The Eye of the Hunter

"You know them. You know what they're like," she says without lifting her head, without looking at me.

A child grown up too soon? A woman.

In a low, bitter voice, she goes on, "I'm not looking for trouble. I don't want to stir up a lot of trouble for myself. Or worse, have my throat slit or even . . ."

Those buttocks, those breasts under the thin cotton shift. A woman. Keeping my eyes fixed on the terraces that rise up beyond the ridgeline, I'm only half listening. First there is that shallow, bare dip that slopes up from here and flattens out into an equally bare platform, ending abruptly over there in that rocky outcrop. Then above, pointing in all directions, the roof beams of the white-washed mud terraces. The better part of the village tips down and out of sight on the other side of the slope. I'm just a stranger here.

Her head bowed, she goes on in that same tone, that same voice, ". . . be left with my guts hanging out!"

She repeats, "You know them. I don't want to stir up a lot of trouble for myself," and her resentful, stubborn face turns a brick-red. It is nevertheless a nice face, with that blue tattoo mark on the forehead.

I let out a string of insults.

And her sole reaction is to raise her head. Lifting it up — those panther eyes of hers are devouring me, defying me too — she steps backward. I follow. Gradually, almost imperceptibly, she reaches a dense clump of cactuses. Monstrous yellow warts of already ripe, pulpy fruit riddle the stumps of green flesh. I pause, very briefly, to glance again toward the houses, or what can be seen of them — still no one. And when I turn back to take another step, Lord Almighty, her smoldering eyes block the way.

1

Perched high in the rocks, surrounded by cactuses and wild olive trees, we stand staring at each other. Like an ardent sea of chalk, the flat plain glimmers far below.

She starts in again: "They'll leave me with my throat cut."

She sizes me up unblinkingly. My insults didn't phase her in the least. Her blazing eyes are still throwing up the same wall, a wall that prevents me from taking another step.

Poised to scream, tempted to do so but checking herself, she says again, "With my throat cut or my guts hanging out, and if my assassins can't finish the job alone, all the others will be there to help them! And who would be to blame? A vagabond, a pig who goes around sticking his nose where it doesn't belong."

"Good God, where is the man?" I ask.

"There, behind the cactuses."

No longer a child, and even less a woman, she motions briefly to one side with her chin.

"He's sprawled back there like a slab of meat set out for curing, an old fleabag that wanders about from hut to hut begging. And once his belly's full, he goes back there, flops down, and spends hours sleeping it off. He saw everything."

I don't know who I'm dealing with anymore. A child? A woman?

"Are you sure?" I ask.

A hoarse laugh cracks in her throat.

"Of course I'm sure! I tell you, he knows everything. And now he's back there snoring on the other side of those cactuses. He'll probably sleep till *aaçer*."

"And you brought me here . . ."

"He comes every day, and who knows him? Not a soul. And he doesn't know anyone either. He's like a lone dog. A stray animal, that's all he is."

Her voice trails off until it finally fades in with the mutterings of the wind, telling its own tale with the very same intonations. I am engulfed in those fiery eyes that are staring relentlessly into mine. A beauty that will cost me dearly — not a child, a woman.

I repeat, "And you brought me here . . ."

Whether it is the wind or the voice, the plangent, sinister complaints persist, ignoring my remark. "If anything happens to me, if the slightest thing ever happens to me — "

Abruptly, I put a stop to it, saying, "What could happen? We'll find out soon enough."

She drops her crazed lament, but immediately affects a mocking tone of voice and asks, "When will we find out? When they come after me? We'll find out when it's already too late?"

"We have the whole afternoon ahead of us. There's plenty of time."

A furtive look lights her face.

"The afternoon. This afternoon?"

And she decides she will venture the question, such a strange question: "Even so, do we really have all that much time?"

With a laugh, trying to look on the bright side of things, I explain, "The shadow of that olive tree is making a perfect circle around its base. It will take quite some time for it to grow long, stretch out away from the tree. When the shadow reaches the horizon, or gets close, the animal, if he is back there, had better wake up. It'll be high time by then."

With her mouth gaping open, she is gulping in the scorched air, shouting, "Oh yeah, sure! And in the meantime, we mustn't disturb his lordship!"

She stifles her cry, avidly swallowing in more air as though there wouldn't be enough. Her wide eyes dart frantically about again.

After a quick glance in the direction of the village, she adds with an anxious yelp, "It'll be too late!"

"Too late?"

Standing there face to face, we can't take our eyes from one another. Sweat is making her hair stick to her temples, dampening her underarms. Drowning in each other's gaze, neither of us utters a word. The virulent, glaring heat, the shrill trilling cicadas, the vi-

3

cious pulsing air, and . . . nothing more. Nothing as far out into the land as one might search.

Simply asking, what is it? . . . what do you have in mind that you . . . ? is like lifting the weight of a mountain.

Exhausted from the effort, I leave the question hanging.

She too, though she doesn't seem to have waited for me to ask before proffering a pat answer, barely has the strength to say, "Because . . ."

As the space filled by the fire spirits grows, the silence deepens, becomes heavier, if that's possible.

Breathing slowly, her parched lips slightly open, she is still casting a dark look at me. Is she aware of it? Does she even see me? I'm not really sure. Then I understand — no, she and I both understand — that, in spite of the silence, there are still words being exchanged between us. The same secret words echoing deep in our flesh, deep down in this dark well, the same fatal words that have already said everything, already pronounced the sentence.

Exasperated, I throw my knife at the trunk of the olive tree. The point sinks into its bark. The blade vibrates, sending the sun reflecting riotously in all directions. And just as it had stuck fast in the trunk, it now grows suddenly still.

The girl turns her head, sees it, then gives me a knowing look. "I'm not looking for trouble."

Her tongue is thick. She moves it with great difficulty, begins talking, like someone who isn't quite all there and doesn't really know what she's saying. "I saw him coming. He was climbing that slope back there, just like you always do, and I thought it was you at first. I was sitting down by these cactuses, and I was waiting for you to come over the top. But, God have mercy, instead I saw him clambering up, leaning on his stick. He was even down on all fours, just like this."

She throws herself down on her hands and knees, scratching at the earth with her fingernails. She's definitely a strange girl, there's no question about that. My patience is beginning to wear thin.

Now her voice is muffled, coldly flat: "You should've heard what he said to me then. He knows everything."

And, still in that crawling position, she begins moving forward, creeping up, coming so close that I can feel her long, slow breath on my sandaled feet. Instinctively, I draw them away. Then I yank the knife out of the tree and she backs off.

In fact, it only seems as if she has shrunk away. She hasn't changed places and, with her mouth almost in the dust, she growls again: "Listen, I don't want to stir up a lot of trouble for myself."

I observe those handsome hips, the snakelike back. I didn't catch what she said after that. But her voice is still drifting up from the dust, and I hear, "What do you plan on doing with that knife of yours? All you ever do is show it off or play with it. I've known you had it for ages now. It's a lovely, long knife, but so what?"

Is she expecting an answer? I don't have one to give her. There is no answer.

She goes on talking into the dust and finally ends up wallowing around in it, "You're always gazing at it as if you could see your own life and soul in that blade. Fondling it, admiring it as if it were in fact your very soul."

I laugh — I can't help it — and in laughing I think, "Something is going to happen, something inevitable, maybe even something irremediable."

The trunk of an olive tree standing there, the trunk of a woman lying there. At least something that won't be in such a hurry to happen as long as we wait here, a nightmare from which we would like to convince ourselves it would be a shame if we didn't wake up in time. A nightmare that only muted, cautious sounds may enter. Sounds? At what point did the girl, stretched out full length at my feet, start laughing too? Or what, sobbing? I try to recall. I don't know how long these hiccups, this insistent wailing, have been going on, how long her body has been racked with tremors like this.

With a quick flick of the knife, I slit the greenish surface of an arm of the cactus. A nauseating, colorless slime oozes from the torn welt of spongy, white flesh.

At the sight of it, I lose control and begin slashing deep gashes in other arms, then still others.

The girl's spasms of hilarity — or despair? — suddenly vanish. Yet it doesn't keep her sides from twitching, her breath from wheezing with a deathly rattle that it seems nothing can still. Just then the heat clamps a leaden mask down on my face, a ringing sound fills my ears. The blinding light flooding down from the sky rips through me, right down to the very roots of the nerves.

I lean back against an olive tree. Not the one which my newly thrown blade has just penetrated, where it is lodged. Not that one — the other one facing it, at the foot of which I contemplate, in dazed horror, the confused tangle of cactus limbs armed with ivory spines while watching the girl who has begun crawling forward again, rhythmically thrusting her pelvis and her hips into the ground.

She is writhing around dragging her body through the dust, gradually closing in on me. She's going to bump up against my legs again. Going to? She's already got hold of one. Her arm is wrapping around it, and something even thicker than the slimy juice of the cactuses is surging through my veins.

When I try to pull my leg free, I realize I can't move at all. Her heaving, torrid breath is blowing on my feet, and there's nothing I can do. It's impossible to break away, impossible to expel the ground glass of sunlight from my eyes. I am still totally stunned. I stand there, rooted to the spot, simply stand there. Frantic, flaming waves are washing over me. My head sways to and fro in the whirling fury of fire.

Her dry, cracked lips come gently to rest against my leg and the horizon turns red. It's not that the sun is ready to go down, it is simply a warning.

And someone pulls the knife out of the tree trunk it was stuck in. Not I — someone else, the unknown hunter. The one who's come up without anyone really asking him to.

The one who doesn't need any particular space to exist or move around in — he fills all space. He goes through doors as easily as air.-The one who crops up in as many different places as can be imagined and in just as many different directions.

At times we can catch a glimpse of him if we want to, springing up out of nowhere and then suddenly vanishing from sight, becoming invisible.

Behind the thick growth of cactuses brandishing their needles, the vagabond lifts himself to a sitting position, looks around. His fist closes tightly over the stick by his side. Sleep's deep creases still remain stamped into the bronzed chaos of his face. The two red and swollen rims of his slightly parted eyelids ooze with rheum.

He pushes himself up from the ground using his free hand and his stick. It's a difficult process for him to straighten up, get himself into a standing position. It leaves him breathless and panting.

But as soon as he is on his feet, the vagabond moves off with a hasty, stooping gait. Without looking back.

The vagabond flees, and the unknown hunter begins the chase. Foolishly believing he has a chance, the vagabond dodges, feints, and, wrapped in his rags, is like a cornered hyena — nothing but a wild animal. An animal with no way out, an animal that can only turn and make its last stand, baring its teeth, gnashing out on all sides.

And its blood came gushing out, and the avid flies, the sun, the dust drank it in. A bloated face that has already turned black like some lightning-charred remnant.

Now the sun will commence its descent. In this utterly desolate world, the dying day has hollowed out an even greater emptiness. Will it be shortened, that path the hunter must take to regain the stillness, the weightless sleep of the stone shed just the time of one brief passing? Shortened, the path along which he can escape the

7

changes that lead to decay? What is behind that rampart of cactuses? And beyond, out past those ragged peaks? That eternal place where evil revels in its own invention, waiting to emerge and shoot out its rays like a second sun?

It matters little to the dust, the rocks, or the wind whether their thirst is quenched with a drop of river water or a drop of blood that will turn the earth red from one end of the valley to the other, the earth that at this very moment turns its hunched back to the unflagging onslaught of winds. The earth, bathed in the silent deluge of molten lava from a punctured sun, takes on the opacity, the stiffness of lead, and the sky too, turning a deep purple, has the color and consistency of lead.

Calmly, I watch, listen. The girl is gone. Will someone find a word one day, the right word to name this vast hemorrhage, and curse the earth for its eagerness to accept as much blood as we might offer it? What's become of that girl?

One earth, one sun, one loneliness, and the long howling that the dogs have begun, lifting their heads toward the red sky where bats, like dark thoughts, flit madly about, knocking frantically against the walls of an invisible prison.

The Detour

"What's a measly hundred miles with the set of wheels I got? Nothing — a mere spin."

The sun was going down, and Ben Mrah was still driving through the outskirts of the large coastal city. He was heading out, with the girl, Soraya, sitting in the passenger seat next to him.

"This Mercedes, the one you're sitting in, is the greatest, the top of the line. It's goddamned out of this world! Hell knows how much I paid for it! Five times what it costs in the country it's made in. No matter what they say, you can get hold of whatever you want here — all the classiest things. You just have to be ready to cough up for it. But, what's the price of a damn car like this to me? Nothing — a technicality. Need a light for your cigarette, Soraya? See that button there? Push it in, it'll pop back in just a second, then pull it out, and presto, you got a light."

Ben Mrah could have bought ten, even twenty cars like this if he felt so inclined. Yet he recalled how he had, like an ass, seriously weighed the pros and cons before finally buying the Mercedes and, for a long time afterwards, had continued driving around in his old junk heap, a total wreck. That's right, he, the fearless deal-maker, who turned such a pretty profit, had actually hesitated. As though he first had to chuck his whole stinking life out the window (the life which should have been irrelevant now), and in a sense, write off the twenty-five years of his previous existence, which had been nothing but an endless string of misery but which was relevant all the same. And he'd broken down. And because of that, he'd vowed to write off his past, had firmly made up his mind never to look back again.

Just thinking back on it made him wince, how pitiful he'd been. He laughed as he pictured this guy perched up there on a pile worth his own weight in gold yet not daring to live the lifestyle his hard work had entitled him to. When that fear grips you, it's a goddamned curse. How could he bring himself to dip into the bread he'd stowed away — break into his capital — and risk being short in the end! Fear had been with him for such a long time, a sickeningly irrational fear that he'd always carried in the pit of his stomach, but then he hadn't known what it was to wear a pair of shoes until the age of ten. A full stomach was rarer still, even after he had grown up, become a man.

So just exactly how did he happen to come into a nice little fortune, to put it politely, at the age of twenty-five? Hold on now, let's not get too pushy. That's confidential, a private chapter of his life — it's no one else's business. Let's just forget the whole thing. And anyway, he's not the only one who has gone that route in this country. Shit! Just take a good look around!

"Soraya, can you light me up a cigarette too?"

He didn't take his eyes off the road. It was a real pleasure, this road, like a thick carpet, and he was just bombing right along. With this little buggy, it's easy to think you're doing seventy-five miles an hour when you've already hit ninety or a hundred. The motor clipped silently along at full speed. The only sound was that of the wind whipping past. Just like flying. It was difficult to tell if it was making any impression on the girl or not. Sitting in the seat next to him, she remained absorbed in her own thoughts. The steady hum was probably lulling her to sleep.

Hunching a little further down into her seat, she broke the silence and asked, "Can I turn on the radio?"

"Yeah sure, go ahead. That's what it's there for."

After that they drove on in an atmosphere filled with the whining of an electric guitar intertwined with a syrupy voice.

"Cheb Khaled," she said.

Ben Mrah didn't comment. He wasn't listening to that music but to a different, wildly thrilling and intoxicating one: that of the motor. He'd discovered how much pleasure this blasted car could give him, and that was all he craved anymore — it was a real high. When he would go out for a drive by himself, he never listened to music. The song of his Mercedes was enough for him.

Keeping his ear tuned to the purring of the motor, he'd forget his cigarette burning slowly away in the ashtray, leaving a long, unbroken ash. As soon as his hands touched the steering wheel, he could think of nothing other than cars and driving.

The huge, yellow sun, like a monstrous egg yolk ready to burst, was already touching the jagged peaks framed by the right-hand side of the windshield. It was beginning to let its own redness gradually seep out over the rest of the naturally rust-colored, naturally scorched land all the way out to the dusty horizon. The black vein of the road slithered along through the dried blood of these lands dotted with endless tufts of bramble bushes. Sometimes, it would suddenly look like a snake with shiny scales gleaming in the sunlight. At least the unbearable heat of the inferno, beating down relentlessly as you penetrated far into the depths of this monotonous wasteland, remained outside. Sitting in the car with the windows closed and the air conditioning running was like traveling in a cool oasis. And the thought that kept running through Ben Mrah's mind, without him really being conscious of it, was of little importance: "Those German bastards know how to do everything."

Through these increasingly frequent trips of his — much more frequent in fact than he deserved — he had grown familiar with the backcountry. The kind of place that gave you the creeps. It was hard to imagine anything more dismal, anything that could turn you off more, really make your flesh crawl. Luckily, he never had to stop for very long in any of these godforsaken holes. Most of the time, he simply drove through them as quickly as possible. City life: there's nothing like it. Ah yes, city life, goddamn it!

Now, they were on their way back home. He hadn't the slightest idea how little miss Soraya felt about it, but as far as he was concerned, he was very pleased with himself for having spent a wonderful day in the big harbor city. It was almost a capital in its own right, and he felt a tinge of regret at having to leave. But, oh well, that's life! You always have always something or other to regret.

He was also feeling quite pleased with himself for having gotten Soraya out of her hole. She had seen a bit of the world with him — it was quite a change. For her, he had lifted a corner of the veil that she, like so many other girls, did not actually wear but that had nevertheless left an indelible mark on her soul. For at least twelve hours, she'd gotten away from her little roach hole in the small town where they both lived and forgotten about the bearded hypocrites who, on top of everything else, could hardly match up to a real man.

Without turning his head, he glanced furtively over at her. Still withdrawn, curled up on her seat, smoking, she was listening, or maybe not, to the music. He had run into her just a few days ago — she was scarcely more than an acquaintance. He had invited her to be the Mercedes's first passenger, and he still couldn't quite get over it.

It was incredible the way they'd had to secretly slip away early that morning. There'll always be some jerks whose major pastime is spying on everyone else, so the two of them had made their getaway on the sly. The poor girl was trying to make herself as scarce as possible. She was downright hiding. And what excuse had she given her family? It was a complete mystery. He hadn't asked. He hadn't asked if she'd ever gone out with a boy before either or even if she'd ever been out of town. He wasn't at all sure she had.

He burst out laughing. Hell knows why.

"What are you laughing about, Ben?"

"Who, me?"

"You were laughing to yourself."

"No, never mind. Don't pay any attention to me. You know how ideas pop into your head sometimes. Do you like this music?"

"I love it."

He thinks: I'd stake my life on it that she's a virgin and that she's never set foot in a restaurant. The one we went to for lunch was perfect, first rate. Perched up on that rocky cliff with the city, the port, and the beautiful blue sea spread out at your feet: real class. I could hardly believe my eyes. Plus, our table was out on the terrace, set up like a couple of pashas, yes indeed — in the shade of those large parasols, with the maître d' on one side, the waiters on the other, sterling silver, at least three or four glasses per person. Up there in the sea breeze, we couldn't even feel the heat, whereas down in the streets, it was crushing.

I'd never been to that spot before, but someone had mentioned it to me. I happened to remember it and drove the car straight up there. It was a great idea, to say the least.

As for the grub, Soraya had never seen anything like it. Neither had I for that matter. She even tasted the wine — I ordered the very best, a domestic wine, "la Cuvée du Président." She had barely wet her lips before she set it back down. Then, making more of an effort, she fixed her eyes on mine and picked it up again. She drank one or two sips and all of a sudden, I'll be darned if she didn't start giggling!

"Don't hold back," I told her. "Go ahead and laugh to your heart's content. There's no one here but the two of us. We're far from those grim-faced characters who are always rattling off scripture, who wouldn't have done anything different than I have, except they wouldn't have left you a moment's peace and would have raped you the first chance they got. You see the Mercedes over there? It's not far. I'll carry you over to it, if need be. I'm ordering another bottle."

She was doubled up, laughing so hard that all she could do was shake her head no. I thought she was going to keel over.

"Look around you," I said to her. "In this part of the country there are still people who know how to enjoy life."

She nodded in agreement, then gained control of herself and didn't drink another drop of wine.

We were in no hurry to get back. Why should we have rushed? Our little rat hole would wait for us — it wasn't about to disappear, no matter how long it took us to drive home. We spent nearly the whole day up there. I think Soraya really enjoyed it. I wouldn't be in the least surprised if she ended up proving to be a pretty nice girl. We had a wonderful time. But things between us went no further than that, our relationship remained on honorable and courteous terms. Ideally, we should plan on coming back some other time, to seal our friendship.

"Holy shit! What in the hell is that blasted thing? It wasn't there this morning!"

Ben Mrah slammed on the brakes, Soraya pitched forward and was almost thrown through the windshield. Thank God for the ABS! If it hadn't been for that, it would have been just like being in one of those deathtraps you run across so often on the roads. Before they'd left, Ben Mrah had asked her to put on the seatbelt, but Soraya hadn't wanted to be bothered with it. His policy had always been to make it the very first thing he did. Now, she was sitting there all pale, with strands of tousled hair hanging down in her face, looking as if she'd just seen her own ghost or met face to face with death itself.

Ben Mrah glared at the barricade set up across the road. On a downslope and immediately after a curve! Road work. It was a goddamned crime.

He clenched his teeth. "Asses! What asses! It wasn't here this morning. The jerks!"

He threw the car into reverse, started the motor back up, and turned off to the right, following the arrow in the center of the barrier. Still furious, he kept thumping the palm of his hand against the steering wheel.

"What if we had run into that in the middle of the night?" he kept repeating, unable to overcome his rage. "There's nothing to warn you! No lantern, nothing to keep you from running smack into it and smashing up once the sun is down."

Turning to look directly at the young woman, he said, "Do you mind turning off that music?"

14

The same affected, ecstatic vocal runs had been gushing nonstop from the radio the whole time.

Soraya docilely switched off the music.

Ben Mrah was inspecting the route he had taken. It was very narrow: a small country road. It wasn't leading directly west, which was the direction they needed to go in.

"It'll get us there sooner or later," he thought. On the other hand, it wasn't by any means meant for a Mercedes, which to him seemed like a personal affront. Nevertheless, he decided it was acceptable, for at least it was paved. His thoughts ran on, "It'll be interesting to see what happens if two cars of this size need to pass each other. That'll be a laugh."

The ashen light of day lingered for a long time before finally dying out and giving way to a sudden, dense obscurity that the car lights could barely slice through. As darkness rushed in, the landscape seemed to recede into the distance, melt away.

Both Ben and Soraya, who still remained silent, felt terribly oppressed. It was probably only the age-old fear that spawns doubts at nightfall as to whether a new day will indeed be born.

The road was growing steeper all the time. Before them, the twin beams of the headlights tunneled through the night. They hadn't passed a single vehicle since they'd left the main road.

Ben Mrah had slowed down considerably. Sitting there closed up in that car was like being under a bell jar, the dim light of the dashboard lent an eerie glow to their faces. After a little while, it seemed as if time itself had been suspended inside the car.

Finally, hardly recognizing his own voice, Ben grumbled, "This is really getting to be too much. We should have gotten back on the main road long ago."

It was sheer hell. They seemed to be dragging this ominous, pitch-black darkness along in their wake. It was closing in on them — the shafts of light from the headlights shot through it but then were simply swallowed up in the denseness of night.

"Good Lord, you'd think the devil himself was out to raise hell tonight!"

Not the slightest hint of a light out here in this backcountry. Nothing near, nothing distant. No sign of a fork in the road either. No other route came to intersect with the one they were on.

Ben Mrah stared out into the blackness, opening his eyes so wide he felt they might pop out of their sockets.

He suddenly brought his fist down hard upon the steering wheel — as if his prayers had been answered, a crossroads had just loomed into view. Ben pulled to a stop, looked around. He couldn't find anything that remotely resembled a signpost of any kind, even of the most primitive nature, and both roads trailed off into the night.

"Shit!"

He'd hit upon the perfect word for the situation.

Peering out along the beams of the headlights with his forehead plastered up against the windshield, he craned his neck to examine the terrain, trying to decide what to do. No, he could hope for nothing better.

It didn't really surprise him. "It's just like everything else in this country: half-assed, and no one gives a damn!"

He started the engine back up. Soraya hadn't changed positions. Curled up on her seat, she kept quiet. She was just waiting. For what exactly? Who knows? For it all to be over with, maybe. Or for something to happen, and it could have been just about anything. And what if that something had already come to pass, what if they were already in the middle of it? So what? It was none of her business, she would just stay out of it. She had nothing to worry about, Ben wouldn't ask for her opinion. She observed the manner in which he was completely ignoring her presence, keeping his eyes glued to his task of navigation, groping along every step of the way.

Then it suddenly dawned upon her, and her heart skipped a beat: they should already be back home at this hour. Ben decided to turn left. Oh, if only they'd be lucky enough to get back on the

right road! If only this were the right way! Her parents only truly
excelled in one thing, and that was making life miserable for her.

She heard stones flying out from under the wheels, felt the car
lurching over deep ruts, and realized they had turned onto a dirt
track. If that had any particular significance, she had absolutely no
idea what it might be.

Ben Mrah let out a long string of curses, but he continued to
push the Mercedes onward, like a man who was convinced that he
had made the right decision, in spite of everything, and that he
would inevitably get back on track. The going was terribly rough,
but they were headed in the right direction. They must surely have
gotten past the strip of road that had been closed for repairs. Also,
the track wasn't leading uphill any longer — they were driving on
flat ground now, which was a good sign. The Mercedes — bouncing from one pothole to the next, pitching unevenly over large
rocks, crunching them to gravel — was taking an awful beating
though! If those blond-headed manufacturers could only see this,
they'd be pulling out their hair by the handful. He found himself
smiling for the first time since the road block. He slowed down
again.

Cut off from the world in their cockpit with the phosphorescent
dashlights masking their faces, the forced intimacy, far from bringing them closer together, only made them withdraw even more,
become more pensive, slip back into the solitude that is natural to
all human beings.

In the flawlessly black night, mountains, whose sheer mass and
density seemed to have redoubled, besieged them on all sides, and
now a low, muttering sound came rumbling from them. It was also
the night that inspired silence. That was exactly it — something
wild had been awakened, and the Mercedes was acting as a rampart
to protect them against it, something that was creeping inexorably
toward them, following their every move, accompanied by that
deep, resounding groan. But what was protecting the Mercedes?

Suddenly, and with a terrible sinking feeling in his stomach, Ben Mrah realized he had driven into a sandpit. He stopped the car. When he attempted to start it back up a minute later, the wheels spun around helplessly. He tried throwing it into reverse; the wheels still spun. He tried again. Nothing worked, the tires just whirled frantically around in the same place spattering a shower of gravel and sand against the underside of the car. This infuriated him all the more and he floored the gas pedal in a rage. The tires reacted just as vehemently, but instead of bringing the car out of the pit, they simply dug it down a little deeper.

Leaving the motor running, he paused to gather his thoughts. Trying to drive the car out of the sand himself would be a careless and stupid move — he would only succeed in getting stuck once and for all. He had to avoid that at all costs. All right, fine, but considering the weight of the Mercedes, it would take several men to help push it out of there. Without cursing or even losing his temper, he stepped calmly out into the night.

After the air-conditioned car, it was like being slapped in the face with the heat from a blast-furnace. Despite the suffocating darkness, it was a relief to stretch his legs. Taking in a deep breath, he inhaled the odor of dry, sun-baked stone. A subtle fragrance of sage and thyme mingled with it. Filled with stealthy, mysterious, barely audible noises, at least the night was alive: the veiled, dark air was vibrant. Ben Mrah strained his ears, not really listening for anything in particular. He peered into the depths of the night, buttressed, thickened by the diaphanous sky like a bucket full of shimmering stars. He had never seen anything like it before — this was a whole new experience. Or maybe it wasn't, in truth. It was just that it left him completely indifferent. To him, the only thing it meant was the problems it would bring.

"Get out of here?" he grumbled. "Get out of this dead-end place, this godforsaken hole? How?"

He climbed back into the driver's seat.

"So, what do you think about all this?" he asked the young woman.

How strange his voice was! It was too high-pitched in contrast to the sound of the motor that was barely purring.

"You're the one who should know, Ben. If I don't get home tonight, I'll be in for it."

Though she had been careful to say that in a neutral tone of voice, Ben Mrah let out a cackle.

"You have no idea what I've already got coming to me, do you? What a mess I'm in as it is? Just sitting here stuck like this with no idea what to do, isn't this just about the worst mess you can imagine?"

"Let's try pushing it."

He responded with the phoniest, most sarcastic laughter he could muster. He switched off the motor that was idling uselessly.

"Do you know how much a Mercedes weighs?"

"No."

"Then let's just drop the subject."

He got back out of the car and stood up to face the night, observing it in silence. The legions of shadows thickened and piled into bastions as high as the sky. He shuddered — what was lurking out there? Not even the sound of a barking dog escaped.

The young woman got out in turn, and the noise of the slamming car door made her jump. Ben Mrah had felt his heart leap into his mouth.

In silence, they stood on either side of the car contemplating the only thing they could, that which lay before them and which they weren't at all certain they wanted to confront.

Then, spontaneously, Soraya began to call out: "Hey-oh! Hey-oh!"

Startled, Ben turned toward her.

"What are you doing? Why in the hell are you yelling like that?"

"Someone might hear me and come and give us a hand."

"Someone hear you? You must be nuts."

Then he changed his mind and mumbled, "Yeah, sure. Why not, after all? You're right to call for help. You're right. . . . Unless someone happens to come and slit our throats."

Soraya's vocal exercises simply echoed out into the vast emptiness, which made them seem all the more incongruous.

Standing there, unable to move, with all of their senses alert, they simply waited.

"Ben, Ben! Can you come over here? This way, Ben!" exclaimed the girl once again, but she was barely whispering this time.

"Now what?"

Insistently, eagerly, she urged, "Come see!"

"What do you expect me to see in this black furnace?"

As soon as she felt him by her side, she took his arm.

"Over there! Just look. That's a light out there, isn't it?"

To humor her, he squinted out in the direction that her hand — barely visible itself — was pointing. There was definitely a bright pinpoint flickering at the top of what must have been a slight rise, a slope in the land.

He immediately expressed his doubts: "It could just as well be a star as anything else! A rising star, or one that is setting. It's so damned dark, you could imagine whatever you like."

"You think that's a star?"

"I said that it could be just about anything."

"And what if we walked over in that direction, Ben? What if we tried to find out? Just to make sure. We might run into some people over there, who knows? Some nice people who just might help us out. What do you say, Ben?"

Might the girl be right? He watched the small point of light blinking in the distance — trying to discern if it was simply an optical illusion or, worse, some kind of trap. His very livelihood often depended upon his being aware that life is full of surprises, that nothing could be trusted, that one should never let his guard down.

After having remained silent for a few minutes, he finally conceded, "We've got nothing to lose by walking over there. But do you really want to come with me? Wouldn't you rather wait in the car?"

"No, I'm coming too, Ben," she answered hurriedly.

He locked up the Mercedes and they set out, keeping their eyes on the tiny flame — or whatever it might be — the only one of its kind, pinned to the black background. It was damn near impossible to estimate the distance that separated them from it.

Soraya was trotting along so close to Ben that she kept bumping up against him with her shoulder or elbow. Also, the path was full of bumps and ruts. It wasn't the easiest surface to walk on, and she was constantly stumbling and tripping.

Ben found the perfect calm, the utter silence of this night just as disturbing as the morass of total obscurity that they seemed to be wading through. Even the sky, a black kettle in which diamonds had been set to boil, did not alleviate the thick gloom about them. But Ben moved forward all the same and, oddly enough, encountered no resistance, except for the insecurity he felt at putting one foot in front of the other in the dark.

How long had he and Soraya been groping along in that manner? Maybe ten minutes at the most when the young lady apparently found nothing better to do than cry out and suddenly dive for the ground.

"Now what's happening?" growled Ben.

That dark voice, a voice as black as the night, was all that came from his mouth.

"It's my shoes. I sprained my ankle."

Clinging to one of Ben's hands, she was feeling her ankle — or rubbing it — Ben, who had stopped, couldn't be sure.

He wondered, "And what about those other twittering sounds that come boring through the night, echoing endlessly out into infinity. The sounds we think are made by crickets, what if the stars themselves made them?"

"That's all we needed. Take them off and walk barefoot."

"On these stones?"

"Then stay here. I'll come back for you later. You'll see, it will only take a few minutes."

For no particular reason, he suddenly imagined his car racing along the highway with the headlights sucking in everything that whipped up in front of them.

"No, I'm going with you. If you think I should take them off — there, I've done it."

Standing back up, she took a few steps clutching Ben's shoulder and limping. Before long, she even let go of him, trying to keep up on her own and walk with as sure a foot as he.

A few minutes later, she began crying quietly.

Ben Mrah hadn't noticed at first, but when he finally did, he pulled her over to him, shaking her gently. Then, little whimpering sounds escaped from her throat. Although he couldn't see her any better than she could him, the utter distress he could feel in the body that was trembling in his arms was heart-rending.

"Poor girl, you've had it already, and we don't even know whether or not we're headed straight into the mouth of hell. Or even whether we'll find anyone or anything wherever it is we are going. Why don't you wait here for me?"

"Ben, please, don't leave me alone."

He decided she'd probably spilt her share of tears for the time being, and that she'd refrain from shedding any more. She was pretty brave, after all. He fumbled around for her arm and grabbed her by the elbow. Helping to support her that way, he urged, "Come on, steady now!"

Groping their way along, they set out again with renewed hope. Since early that morning, Soraya had been relying upon Ben for everything. She certainly didn't intend to stop now. And he was relying on his *baraka* — that was the word he kept repeating to himself — never imagining for an instant that his lucky star might abandon him. No matter how dire the straits, he never lost his head. He'd rather be torn limb from limb than allow his fears to get the better of him. He admitted that the situation seemed ominous, even treacherous, that it was quite possible that some kind of danger was lurking out there in the night somewhere, waiting for them, if it hadn't been following them from the moment they had started out in the morning. He didn't deny any of that — he was even under the distinct impression that it was the case. All the same, he vowed to get through this, come hell or high water.

Like a sleepwalker spurred on by a paradoxically blind yet clairvoyant force, he stumbled forward without allowing himself to look back. Therefore, he didn't see the strange halo that the headlights of his Mercedes cast into the night sky. He managed to forget about Soraya herself, even though he was holding her up as she walked. Totally detached from himself, his steps were driven by only one idea, to somehow get his car back on the road.

It was like being startled out a of a dream when he and the young woman ran smack into an obstacle that responded with a deep grunt: "Just where do you think you're headed there?"

Grabbing the thing that had spoken with both hands, Ben prepared himself for a fight.

"Calm down, friend," said the voice again.

The man, obviously taller and stronger than Ben, seized him in turn by both arms and easily pushed him away.

"So, you want to start a fight without even invoking name of the Almighty?"

The peasant's voice seemed to be coming from a deep barrel, muffled and slow, and there was a sarcastic ring to it.

"What are you looking for over this way, friend? And in the company of a child as well! There's nothing out here. Nothing but our village, just over that way."

The man in the shadows remained silent, awaiting a response. When he didn't get one, he repeated, in the same calm tone of voice he had used at first: "And with a child too! Come along, both of you. May it never be said that guests led to our very doorstep by Providence were turned away. Our *douar* is just a short walk from here. Do you see that line of hills over there? It's right behind that."

A line of hills? Where? Ben tried to make it out, but the derisive opacity of that diabolical night only seemed to accentuate the *fellah's* unspoken scorn.

Then the man began to caution them — one would have thought he were reeling off a litany: "You'd best follow me. If you'd gone any closer, I can guarantee the dogs would have torn you to pieces. The ones that guard our village don't bark, even after they've attacked.

This time the man let out a sort of snicker that ended in a sound something like that of an eggshell being crushed.

Still not having recovered from his surprise as he stood there in the dark, Ben was trying to decide how to save face and, steadying his voice, said in a condescending tone, "Our automobile, we left it back there, we need . . ."

"Is that a child you've got with you?"

"We need some help, just a few people to push us out. A child? No. With several people pushing . . . There's nothing wrong with it, a Mercedes, it's simply stuck in the sand and needs to be pushed out, that's all."

A pair of rough, callused hands took hold of Soraya and began feeling her face, her neck, her shoulders. "Damned if it's not a woman!" the great, loutish *fellah* exclaimed. "Say now, that's a woman you've got there, and you just drag her about wherever you like? How did you happen to wander into this godforsaken place?"

"Just a small push would be enough to get it out of the sand. It's right back there, just a little way down the path."

"Since you say it's not far from here, there's nothing to worry about. It can sit there for a hundred years, nothing will ever happen to it. I can swear by that!"

Because they were standing there talking to each other in the dark, Soraya was under the impression that somehow neither of the men were talking in the right direction, that one man's voice didn't always reach the other's ears, and that with each remark they were turning their heads and would raise their voices in an attempt to bridge the immeasurable distance between them.

In his drawling accent, choosing his words carefully, the spectral peasant was explaining to them: "All you need to do for the time being is just walk a little bit further and we'll be there, you'll see."

"On these rocks and in bare feet!"

The complaint had escaped Soraya's lips, and, standing stock still, she went on, "I can't go another step! Go ahead and do whatever you like, but I can't take another step! Just leave me here. I'll wait for you to come back."

Unless she'd been mistaken, her words had been met by a snide little laugh.

"I never heard a woman talk so much, especially not one who seems to be so little! Wait for what? Come along, little woman!"

As if she were as light as a feather, Soraya felt herself being lifted from the ground by two terrifyingly muscular arms, and soon afterwards she thought she would suffocate in those same arms, overwhelmed by the smell of sweat and earth mixed together.

The *fellah* was also sniffing, and he remarked in his bellowing voice, "Oh my, the lady certainly smells sweet, just like a bouquet of flowers."

In a flash, Ben Mrah realized what had happened. He couldn't think of an appropriate remark to make, so he simply remained silent.

A little later, he heard the young woman exclaim, "Stop! I lost one of my shoes. It fell out of my hands!"

Phlegmatically — one might even say fatalistically — the *fellah* boomed out over her protestations: "Don't you worry, little woman, wherever it fell, it isn't lost. Nothing gets lost in these parts. We can always come back and get it when it's daylight.

Daylight! What kind of a nut was he to think they would be spending the night out in these mountains? Not on your life! It was unthinkable!

Being carted around like that made her feel like one of those young lambs that the shepherd had to carry because they were too weak to walk. She held her breath, imagining it would help make her lighter and thereby minimize the contact of his arms around her.

They had apparently just skirted the line of hills he had pointed out, for rather than a pack of dogs, a drove of fiendish beasts suddenly rushed out, crowding and jostling one another in the dark, to surround the little party. In a fury, they were all foaming at the mouth, snapping, growling. Not one barked. It would have been less horrifying had they barked.

Soraya could feel herself bobbing up and down as the *fellah* kicked out at the beasts, to the front, to the side. He cursed them, shouting at the same time: "Down! Stay!"

Soon, the young woman could make out dim, wavering white shapes looming up through the night and recognized — or thought she recognized — sections of wall standing at different levels. Houses! Just as the man had said. Built into the side of the hill, each set a bit higher than its neighbor, approximately five or six houses stood intently observing the strangers.

"That's what I saw glimmering from afar," thought the girl to herself with a grim sort of satisfaction.

The dogs were definitely backing off, but they were by no means turning tail, making a run for it, returning to whatever dark hell had vomited them up. Maybe in their crazed tenacity, they still hoped to tear the visitors to pieces. And how much darker, how much longer, could this night grow?

Just then, the *fellah* scrambled up the side of an embankment and in a few strides, carrying his burden, sidled through a narrow door that seemed to swing open on its own.

As is the custom for men, Ben Mrah stopped at the threshold. He waited there and heard the peasant announce, "Look what I've brought back for you."

It was clear that there were women inside the house. One of them finally decided to ask, "Sugar and tea. Besides that, did you get anything else?"

"Yes, of course, don't worry. Please come in! You don't intend to spend the evening outside, do you?"

Not in the least surprised at having been so heartily invited, Ben stepped into the house. A strong smell of mildew, like in a cellar, mingled with the smell of burning kerosene immediately engulfed him, and he was half-blinded by the flame of a lantern that was barely bright enough to reach all the way to the back of the long room where he found Soraya standing on her own two feet and grinning!

The *fellah* was still in the process of taking the rucksack from his shoulder when a big strapping young woman, tanned and as solidly built as he was, came and held out her hand to take it. Dwarf-like, the slumping shape of another woman could be distinguished back in the shadows.

Seizing the rucksack, the first woman went on, "And you've brought that back with you too?"

"That's right," said the peasant, answering her as only a husband would, which is what he undoubtedly was. "I ran into her on my way home."

Silently, without being in the least concerned with what Soraya might think, the woman reached out and touched the girl with her free hand. Apparently, it was less to make sure that Soraya was real than to have the pleasure of touching her dress, or rather, the fine material it was made from.

Very quickly, however, and with disarming frankness, she observed, "She's completely naked underneath."

The young woman, who had not shied away or even moved, suddenly turned red. The *fellah* looked the other way. At the edge of the circle of light, the slumped form — and it was not a dwarf at all but an old woman sitting on the floor with her legs doubled up underneath of her — began making signs in Soraya's direction. But the *fellah*'s wife had already taken charge of the girl.

"Follow me," she ordered.

The two women disappeared into an adjoining room — or was it a pantry?

As for Ben, he was wondering why anyone would use a lamp that sputtered and dwindled and threw out such a dim, reddish light. It was such an ancient object — he'd never seen anything like it before. The light was nowhere near as bright as he'd believed it to be at first.

The old woman continued to make signs, pointing to the empty place beside her on a goatskin, which she now offered to Ben, who didn't notice at first. After quite a long while, he finally became aware of it, and without understanding, began to observe the hand that kept motioning to him. Only then did he think to look at the woman as well — her dark gaze seemed to glow with a mysterious light.

None of this made him feel very comfortable. He had already planned out exactly how he would go back to the car, followed by several strong fellows from the village. He had imagined the Mercedes being pushed out of the sand . . . And here he was standing before an old peasant woman lost in a pile of rags. However, apart from wondering what he should do next, which provoked a flood of useless conjecture, he could think of nothing better to do. No, nothing, since events seemed to be following some sort of preconceived plan without anyone having anything to do with it at all.

The *fellah* had left him there, gone over to rummage around in a corner, and then walked out of the room carrying an earthenware pitcher. Soon afterward, the sound of splashing water could be heard.

Soraya entered the room again, walking ahead of the woman of the house. She was almost unrecognizable, draped in an ample peasant dress with colors that flashed and danced despite the now murky light of the lantern. Then the man came back. He paid no attention to Soraya. Walking past Ben Mrah again with his earthen-

28

ware pitcher, he indicated, with a jerk of his chin, the spot on the goatskin that the ancient lady had offered him. But the old woman had already turned her mute appeals on Soraya who, seeming to focus exclusively on her gesticulations, accepted. The *fellah*, still without uttering a word, pointed out another skin to Ben, a sheepskin, spread out near the opposite wall. Ben had no choice but to do as he was told and sit down. His legs would barely hold him up any longer.

*

Suddenly, his eyes opened. His gaze fell abruptly upon a wall daubed with blue paint. It was daylight. It was daylight and here he was lying down with his nose against this wall. Would he come to in the same place that he had dropped off to sleep? Would he be able slip back into his body? The only things it was letting in for the moment were the crisp chill and the sharp light that seemed to be all the morning was made of. But the chill and the light were still struggling against warm drifts of lingering night floating about here and there. From somewhere, the rhythmic splash of waves, sea foam blinking out as it soaked into the sand. For the time being, the present had no future, no past.

Then everything came back to him: the road, the detour, the Mercedes getting stuck in the sand, the trek through the night, and the way he had allowed himself to fall asleep on a sheepskin in that very same spot on the floor. He turned over. His ribs ached. So now he was going to be sore all over. Not far from him, the ancient lady, sitting on her legs just as he'd left her the night before, started motioning to him in hurried, nondescript hand signals as soon as he turned toward her. Also, she was laying her hand on her cheek, tilting her head to one side, which obviously could only mean one thing: "There's nothing to keep you from sleeping a little longer, son." Unless she was congratulating him for having slept so well. He thought it would be best to sit up. Settled into this new position, he put his arms around his knees and suddenly realized: this old peasant woman was using sign language with him because she didn't

29

believe that they spoke the same language. That was it . . . a different language . . .

Then, the *fellah's* wife came in, but only to set down a pot covered with a large slice of flat barley cake in front of him. Just as they had the night before, the deep, still pools of her eyes, under their dark browline, punctuated by the *harkous*, seemed to unknowingly engulf her whole face without leaving a ripple.

"And Soraya? Where has she gone off to?"

While still stooping, the woman started and shrank back in fright, as if she couldn't believe her ears. He had spoken to her. She had understood and was absolutely baffled. It must have been as puzzling to her as it was to the old woman. In answer to his question, she pointed to the door, through which she herself then furtively disappeared, leaving him just as perplexed as before.

"Outside, but where?"

In the meantime, gesticulating eloquently from where she sat, the grandmother was entreating Ben to taste the food that had just been brought to him. He picked up the flat cake and discovered the pot underneath to be full of thick, creamy milk.

He was still partaking of his frugal meal under the old woman's watchful eye when the tall form of a young peasant came to stand in the doorway, blocking out the light. Without even being able to make out his features, Ben immediately recognized their guide and savior of the previous night. The man refrained from taking another step forward. Standing there on the doorstep, he shook out a piece of cloth that hung all the way down to the ground between his two hands. Puzzled by his strange behavior, Ben didn't understand at first, didn't see what their host was driving at. Then in the very same instant, it became evident: the man was waiting for him to get to his feet, which is what Ben did, abandoning the rest of the bread and milk. The musclebound *fellah* immediately draped a lily-white burnoose over his shoulders. After that, with his hand behind Ben's back, he guided him through the door, out into the sunlight.

Another slight nudge from that same hand sent Ben tripping

down toward the first of the five or six houses. Unlike its neighbors, this house was built on a flat terrain. He was walking along mulling the whole situation over in his mind, worried — but not all that much really — about what was happening to him, the attention he was getting. Did he find this to be a normal course of events? No, not really. Everything here was extraordinary in one way or another. He wasn't looking for answers and he wasn't about to ask any questions.

Wait and see. They rounded the corner of the house and he saw. It was a miracle that they didn't trip over the *fellahs* gathered there, some squatting and others actually sitting cross-legged, on straw mats *as if they were expecting him*. He was shocked, to say the least. Who were all these people? They seemed to be waiting to take part in some kind of ceremony.

Despite the fact that this place simply held no answers, some of Ben's questions warranted one, especially considering all the new things he was discovering with every step. In the end, it was his instinct that warned him: there was definitely something strange going on here. The men were preparing to honor him in some way. It neither embarrassed nor troubled Ben, but he was overcome with a feeling of absurdity. Utter and indescribable absurdity was also what he felt just a moment later when he noticed the scene before the crowd: an idol covered with a veil, a phantom sitting on a painted chest and leaning up against the wall of the house. Great gods, it was Soraya! He recognized her in a flash. The immaculate, white *haïk* enveloped her from head to toe.

Ben tried to think. The fact that she was here too meant they would take part in it together, but take part in what exactly? Damned this village and the people in it! A welcoming ceremony? Some kind of ritual practice? A double homage? Now he really did want to know. He was racking his brains again when his patron, his chaperon, in the same kindly fashion, led him over toward the young woman and pressing — still ever so gently — upon his shoulders, seated him at her side. A wager? A pretext for playing this game? What did they represent to these people? Ben was puzzled, but he became extremely irritated when he noticed the guide with catlike eyes walk away and, without further ado, slip through the rows of spectators and vanish. What was going on here anyway? What were these people up to? Everyone seemed so serious.

Then, the only figure wearing a yellow turban (a simple white cloth was wound about the heads of the rest of the crowd) launched into the most ludicrous homily that Ben had ever heard: "My dear children, you have been led here by the hand of God. Blessed be the moment you first set foot upon our soil." (The orator made a sweeping gesture with his arm taking in the immensity of the surrounding countryside.) "Our land, as you can see for yourselves, is exactly as it appears to be: arid, barren, desolate. Yet we've toiled unsparingly and without complaint to make it hospitable and productive. Nothing has worked — the only things this land dispenses liberally are misery and affliction."

The middle-aged man poked out his bony, joyless face, blotched with whitish, scaly patches, upon which — in place of a beard — grew a sort of black lichen that threatened to creep right up to his eyes, and dear God, those eyes! Gleaming with a morbid luster, they were both wild and hallucinating, devoured by an eager ecstasy. "Luckily Soraya, protected by the veil, doesn't have to confront that look," thought Ben who, not being so fortunate, held the gaze that seemed to seep up from the darkest imaginable depths.

The sheik, if indeed that was what he was, continued to make his case: "Why are we the expiatory victims of this type of injustice when we offer our prayers up to the heavens with humble and loyal hearts? We have had signs sent to us in answer to that question and they have taught us what we lack!"

Unexpectedly, he sank into a painful silence.

He remained silent, and the air became laden with an indescribable, almost reverent feeling of resignation.

Though the ascetic also seemed somewhat overwhelmed with dread, he mustered all of his courage and went on. All of a sudden, he started back in again with renewed virulence: "What we have

been lacking are mediators!" The cry of hope had been shouted out
so desperately that silence settled heavily back in again. Then, as if in
still another sign of abandon, the thin whistling of the wind floated
forlornly over the quiet crowd.

The sheik made one last attempt, this time in a hushed voice:
"Each *douar* has their mediators. But we do not. Each *dechra* has their
mediators. But we do not. In the cities, there are so many, they lose
count of them. But we don't have a single one. Not a single one."
(With a sweep of his outstretched hand, he once again indicated the
surrounding wasteland.) "And because there are no *mourabitines* to
sleep in these lands, you can see what they have become. I call upon
you to bear witness, you, who have been sent to us by the will of the
Almighty, who have been chosen by his will to be our protectors,
our intercessors. You, whom we will humbly serve."

The aging man's voice broke with a little sob that was as irritating
as the yelp of a lap dog.

"You're completely off beam, you poor, misguided fanatic," Ben
thought to himself. "You've got the wrong people here. You needn't
be explaining all of this to us. If all of your concerted efforts haven't
been able to make a beanstalk grow in this godforsaken country of
yours, what do you expect us — a couple of simple strangers passing
through, who got stuck because of a damned detour — to do about
it?"

The sheik was going on, completely absorbed in his diatribe,
"And so you came. Providence guided your steps toward us and our
poor, barren land. Praise the Lord!" (He cupped his hands together
as if in prayer or in hopes that they would somehow be filled with
unforeseen gifts from heaven.) "You have now become our patron
saints! The All-Merciful in his infinite kindness has answered our
prayers!"

If Ben hadn't been able to control his indignation, he would have
burst out in loud, derisive laughter. This crackpot, unquestionably
an absolute fanatic, was carrying this joke too far. Couldn't he see
that it was all becoming a bit ridiculous?

Ben rose to his feet and said in a confident, loud voice, "What do you want your tribesmen to take us for? The type of saints that will resolve your problems in exchange for lighting a candle on their tomb? That would be a real joke! And we were expecting you to come to our aid!"

The only thing he could think of to do then was to snicker and ask: "If it hadn't been for the detour, things would have turned out differently, wouldn't they? What would you have done then?"

Humbly, the other answered, "But things did not turn out differently!"

Taken aback by this response, Ben didn't quite know why, but he turned toward Soraya. It wasn't to ask her opinion, but as he observed her sitting there under the veil, so completely terror-stricken that she was holding her breath, four giants grabbed him. Four. He struggled with all his might, but he was quickly overpowered and rolled up in the white burnoose. Propping him up, they dragged their burden over to a pit that had obviously been dug during the night — the mound of dirt beside it was still fresh — and pushed him in.

This time, Ben didn't hold himself back — he allowed his great, bellowing laughter to ring out. But before he could dry his eyes, another group of ruffians threw Soraya into the bottom of the pit with him. She landed nearby without uttering a sound, as if she were already dead. Immediately afterwards, a lid made of wooden beams lashed hastily together was pulled over the mouth of the hole. Ben listened as huge boulders were rolled into place over their heads.

Lined up on the long mat, all the men of the *dechra* were praying. Standing, kneeling, bowing to touch their brows to the ground, they humbled themselves before God. As a closing ceremony, their voices rose in what could be taken for a rite of thanksgiving. For a long time their resounding chant could be heard drifting over the land, chiming in with the sound of its own echo as it bounced off the surrounding mountains.

The Little Girl in the Trees

The morning comes. A door swings silently, opens. The world is white. I saw it. One single white page, with no memories. You can draw whatever you like on it. Whatever you like: trees, houses, flowers, the sky and its clouds. Roads leading off in every direction. The world as you would like to see it. But it's best to wait for just a bit. It's best to look at that miracle, that whiteness, that which is already there, that which exists in the beginning. And it should look at you a bit too. Whiteness born of emptiness, whiteness born of silence. Whiteness that seems as though it's on the verge of speaking but does not speak and simply contents itself with being there. The best thing that you, yourself, can do is follow its example and just be there. And if you don't, well, it's just too bad. You might — just might — regret it afterwards. You might well even be ashamed at not having been able to rejoice in that happiness. But what can you expect?

One should always be in the right place. At the right time. Because . . . because that kind of happiness won't wait — it goes quickly by and once it's too late you can't stop things from happening, from taking on their own forms, the way they are supposed to be, the way they want to be. And then you shan't have deserved the whole miracle offered you, at which you've not even deigned to glance.

Also, you either know how to look or you don't — how true! But it doesn't hurt to try. The sooner you go down into your garden, the better your chances are of getting a glimpse of that white page, of finding it unspoiled in all of its splendor.

I look around, and it's true: the night has erased the world so that it can be reborn and so that we can rediscover that page upon which everything can be written anew.

Right in the middle of everything, concentrating as hard as I can, I think: "But who would ever let himself ruin a whiteness so beautiful that even the birds don't dare open their beaks and go into raptures from simply gazing upon it? Who, rather than just filling their heart with it as they do? — Would I?

"I, who am sitting here waiting?

"Why me?"

*

The air has already taken on the gentleness of blue eyes. No one ever asked so much of it, nor so quickly. I'm still watching and waiting, and getting worried about the page that stays white but not for as long as I worry, watch, and wait. The page, which slowly grows less white, stops being white, and when it disappears, God, how lost I feel.

Adieu, lovely whiteness, beautiful silence. Time, sometimes you imagine that it snaps. But no. Filling with things, filling with voices, with people, with animals, the world is already filling itself up with everything. The garden too has gone and changed. There's nothing but trees — they're still keeping quiet. From time to time, they look at you, stupefied, and you wonder why. As for the birds, they haven't waited to start in on their racket. And so, like in a photograph coming to life, all at once, the leaves start rustling. A breath of air, even the very lightest one, will go and turn them all up on you. If, in addition to that, it blows them up into the rising sun, they'll suddenly go and change from the green that they appear to be, that they show on the outside, into quivering golden flames.

And so the summer hangs up its mirrors everywhere, and I, as long as they are dangling there trembling, I tremble just as much. Boy, are they crazy, those mirrors, to be trembling like that for something they don't have.

My apple tree, the one I'm already perched in, is also crazy. Crazy too, at this very minute, is the garden, and crazy, the world — that world which never strays very far, never loses sight of you. You're absolutely normal and then, a second later, you're completely crazy. But otherwise it's beautiful. You can sit there watching the trees that, having woken up now, are rubbing their eyes, and in the meantime, the only thing that you can think of to do is open your own, so you might better see how they are all standing around you, hardly moving. Like being alive and not knowing you're alive.

That's precisely what I'm waiting for — that instant when they finally realize that I'm here and I . . . I close my eyes. For the time being there is nothing but the morning coolness and me, waiting. I close the eyes that I opened six years ago. I close them thinking, "You could never describe such coolness without going deep within yourself and shivering. I'm going to melt. Melt? First I'd better be sure that I really want to." Six years old, and I'm so big already. With their tangy, lively smell, each of these apple trees, birch trees, pine trees, oak trees is my guardian. Even each of these small plants with their faint, hollow smell or the grass with its joyful dewdrop tears. All these things that live for themselves and for us as well.

As soon as my eyelids drop, a curtain lifts, Papa appears, and I feel protected. He's there; there's something mysterious. His eyes aren't looking at me but off to the side at Mama, Mama with her tulip-shaped chin and her smile that looks like a shimmering light over that tulip. He's looking at her more intensely than he ever does in reality — with that kind of pain, that grief you always feel when someone crops up someplace but it's impossible to reach them. And yet, no matter where Mama is supposed to be standing, she's simply standing in the center of the room. He would only have to take a step forward, and they would fall into each other's arms.

But he looks as if he's chained to his work table, while she, standing in the middle of the room, keeps motioning to him to get up, to come to her. And again, that motioning, again that calling with her hands as if it could help him. And he stares at her, and you should just see that look in his eyes — a look, you'd think she was waiting for him beyond the wall that's behind her, beyond the garden, beyond the world.

And why all this motioning? So that he'll dance! Come and dance with her. He shakes his head in the meantime and smiles in the sorriest way, without getting up, without leaving his table.

She begins to dance by herself. For the two of them.

He simply follows her movements with a tormented look.

Neither he nor she know that I'm watching them.

*

It's true. As soon as she hears some music, she's at it again. And there's often music playing — Papa works with the radio on. She dances even when she's busying herself with the housework. She keeps working and dancing. She's got a natural inclination for it. She's a born dancer. And no need for a partner, right now, to accompany her nor an audience to admire her. Some people talk, converse with themselves. Mama dances with herself.

It wasn't the best thing to have seen, but I saw it. From now on, I had better keep my eyes opened.

No, perched up in my apple tree, I'd rather wait a little longer. The garden might forget me for a second, forget that I'm nested up in my tree, because I'm always searching for the power that is in charge of making the world strong and, above all, making me strong. If I find it soon — and I have to find it — I'll ask the garden to be a little patient, just long enough for this burning moment to pass. Loneliness burns too, the loneliness of being left out. But would anyone ever say so? What would there be left to talk about then? Pain? Brutality?

Here I am off hunting, and for the moment, Papa is close behind me. We're penetrating deep into the forest, the palace of these dark soldiers, all decked in white tunics, still, silent. *Birches*, whispers the wind. It says what's standing there, and it says nothing more. But there's all the rest that the word doesn't say, that it keeps to itself, that the forest keeps to itself. And that makes us be as quiet as they are and wonder. Lord, how true it is that every little question asked about the most insignificant grain of sand only leads to another question and never a real answer! Because that's just the way it is, nothing ever gets a real answer. I'm no fool. I understand that if a

single answer were ever given, no one would ever ask another question, no one would ever struggle again to find anything out about
anything. The forest, the trees, just like words, are always making
new questions. Do you know what they do that for, Papa?

"I'm quite aware of it. But awareness of something is not necessarily something that can be expressed."

"Things have never even told us their name, or even if they have
a name, a name they would call themselves."

"Never. And I have the feeling that it doesn't matter to them in
the least that that's the way things are."

"We're always speaking up in their place, and they just let us
babble out the most ridiculous nonsense."

"It's difficult to imagine what a mountain of nonsense that
makes."

We're moving along through the legions standing in close, or-
derly formation, but they are rationing our air. It's impossible for
Papa and I to walk side by side anymore, so I take the lead. Papa, I
think, prefers that. Something is gnawing away at the silence,
gnawing some more: it's the rippling of water, a voice talking to itself off in the distance and, keeping the same distance, moving
along with us.

We're but wolves now, a vague memory informs me of this.
Wolves back in their natural habitat. The forest is the paradise we
once lost. I didn't remember that. This is where we originated. We
lived here. I needed to have Papa with me before I could recall that.
Two wolves with a shared wisdom, the forgotten wisdom that
comes back to you and gives you a name, the wisdom we think is
lost forever, and ourselves lost along with it.

Things will speak of their own accord when they want to. That's
what they're doing right now, all around us. No sense in questioning them or speaking in their place. You just have to trust them and
listen. We're all ears, Papa and I — that's how we learn our lesson
and get a second chance. It's a secret. The same one that was burning a little while ago. Pain, I was saying, brutality.

I could just as well have thought: "Brutality and happiness. Why not?"

We're two wolves, nothing less, and we're running together. And even if this forest isn't paradise, even if it's hell, here we are, the two of us and, as wolves, we can hear the words that are speaking just to us from everywhere and all at once.

Pricking up my ears, I don't care who I am anymore. I no longer need to shout out who I am. This ancestral run, the uppermost thing in our wolf memory, is putting our story — Papa's and mine — back on the right track. But Papa stops.

"Haven't we gone a bit too far?"(He motions to the impenetrable, thick growth of trees.) "Should we keep going?"

"Mïka, Papa! What are you afraid of? I'm right here with you."

I open my eyes wide to hide a smile. Above all, he mustn't notice it. I want these eyes of mine to seem innocent, deep, black, and just as terrifying as they are reassuring.

"Then let's go on," he says.

"Hyvä, Papa!"

I take him off to get lost in this sylvan antiquity, which isn't unfamiliar to him even though he's a stranger here. He'll see, just as I hope to, the wolf-genies we are going to meet. But I think he already knows; he knows everything. So, it's up to me to lead the way through the aquarium-like light and the damp, moldy leaves of the undergrowth. Closer and closer, the birches circle in on us — that same deaf, silent army through which you have to elbow your way forward. Thousands of eyes are watching closely — they don't let you catch sight of them, but you can feel them. A forest can become suddenly enchanted, simply to enchant you. I'm holding my breath — it'll make me invisible.

    *

I blink my eyes. They crack open, open wide. The world rushes up — no forest and not enchanted, only the old friend, the forest that stretches away from our unfenced garden, which has also come back bringing along the flowerbeds planted with rose bushes.

They're in bloom right now, the rose bushes, a deluge of such deep red fragrance you could faint! In the long run, I prefer the gooseberries to them. Already, scores of them are growing red, tiny bunches of sweet-sour pearls wink at you through the lush tangle of stems and leaves. A bee. I get as drunk as a bee sucking on those sweet little hearts. There are so many things like that, things that are concerned for our well-being and want nothing more than to be useful to us.

Our garden, the forest comes right into it without really being asked — it's at home there. And the garden, from as far away as the forest comes — and that's from very, very far away — welcomes it with open arms. The garden also probably knows very well that I'm sitting up on a branch in the apple tree with my legs hanging down and dangling in the air, beginning to tingle. But isn't my mind tingling just as much with all these thoughts? Even so, I stay right where I am. And wait. Papa points out, "We're always waiting for something."

He's a good one to be pointing that out. I'm always waiting for him to come back, even when he's right here with us, because Papa only comes back long enough to leave us again. After how long? After a while! That's why I don't take my eyes off him: because one second of inattention and, quick as a flash, he's gone. But he's not lost. My eyes keep track of him and follow him out to that place he's always returning to. I don't run after him. I wait. And he comes back. Everything comes back to those who know how to wait: the fathers, the world, the springtime, the roses, the gooseberries, whatever your heart promises itself. And I know how to wait. Why shouldn't I let the object of my desire come of its own free will? Just for a change.

*

The garden is quiet. I'm quiet. Because it's early. Because it lasts a long time. I try to appear to be gazing off somewhere else, and it, I'm sure, is observing the way that I'm scrutinizing things from above. It must be waiting for something too, but what could a garden be waiting for? From up on my high perch, I can make out the marks I left in the sand of the pathways, and I think, "They're the footprints of some visitor, of my other self."

I feel amazed at having recognized them, and being amazed makes me a part of this eternal day, of the eternal me in the green branches of the apple tree, of the eternal light shed by the leaves.

There's nothing but the low hush of the trees when a gust of wind tangles in their limbs to disturb this eternity. And what if eternity itself creates it?

And you keep waiting. Either the greenness will go back to sleep and eternity, wide awake, will continue to stand watch, or the hush will come again and that very instant will be the end of eternity. You'll end up forgetting about it simply from living.

I'll never stop cooking up my own ideas. All sorts of ideas. And I won't forget either Papa or Mama in any of them, Papa and the prayer of his wolf eyes contemplating a lamb.

Now, a rain of live embers is falling. Bouncing through the branches, they scatter about on the garden grass and all over. The leaves are panicking, plagued in this blight. It even seems as though the cars, way out on the road, are frenzied, grumbling, delirious.

As for me, my body is heaving, sweating out more and more heat. Doesn't everyone know that fire thrives on heat? I say to myself, "But it could spread to the garden, to the house with Papa, Mama, and the countless objects that love us and are so devoted to us".

Should I call out? I'm afraid to. Afraid to hear my own voice, to hear it answering me itself. I can sense that one of those machines that crushes everything is nearby. It's turned on right now.

As much of a wolf as I am, I'm going to pray, not to a lamb but to heaven. All that the words need to do is find a way out. I hope they'll find one, and what difference does it make whether it's the mouth or not?

Then Papa's voice comes and immediately afterwards, rising, rising over it, Mama's laughter, like the song of an opera singer, exploding exactly the way it does from the radio sometimes. She laughs marvelously, throwing her head back a little, and in that position, her throat swells out like a pigeon's. I love to see her laugh. What are they doing, those two, that amuses them so much you can hear it all the way up in my tree? Just because they love each other, do they think they're all alone in the world? What about me? I, who have nothing but them, these parents? Have they forgotten me? I'm going to pray for them too, just in case.

I'm looking for the right words. Suddenly a spot of tar appears in the daylight. I hope it won't spread, grow steadily larger until it devours all the light. It had better just stay right there, charred little star that it is. I can hardly go around screaming Help! Help! just because of it. Or feel sorry for it, that strange sort of star, no bigger than a mole's eye, but so completely black.

I jump down from my tree. It's the smartest thing to do. As long as I'm near them, Mama and Papa will keep living, be safe and sound. So in the meantime, I can't go around ending up just any old place. There's a part for me and a part for them. I'm hurrying to go and tell them the good news: that I'm their daughter, that I'm here, they don't have to worry. That's something I've just learned myself. I was more or less aware of it before, when I was still a lost princess. But before is not the same as afterwards.

At the house, I run into Papa.

"Well, well!" he calls out. "Did you just run into the devil?"

And Mama, where's she gone off to? Probably down in the basement taking a shower. She's always taking showers all day long.

"Papa, leave the devil out of this. Do you know that I'm your daughter?"

"There's not a father in the world who knows as well as I do that a girl is his daughter and, knowing that the girl is his daughter, could be any happier, not to mention the fact that he's known it for quite some time. I mean, known she was his daughter."

He's taken off the wolf mask he was wearing. But where did he put it? He's not holding it in his hand.

"That's good," I say.

43

"I think so too."

"But that doesn't keep you from being maybe a little disappointed."

"In what?"

"In the girl that I am."

"There's not a father in the whole world who is happier — "

"You already said that."

" . . . happier to have a daughter like his daughter than I am to have you for my daughter and — "

"Do you really believe that?"

"Yes. And you'll always have something special that no one else has."

"Go ahead, let's hear what this something special might be."

"Yourself."

"All right, but isn't there a simpler way of saying it?"

"Alas, no. If I said it more simply, I wouldn't be the father you have for a father."

"That's the way we are. *Mutta ei se mitään.*"

"Yes, it's just the way we are."

"At least you won't mind dancing with me when I grow up, will you?"

"With you?"

"He hangs on the two words. He takes forever to finish repeating them, "With . . . you . . .""

Now that his lids have stopped blinking, his eyes are glowing with a gentleness only found in wolves. They are brimming with golden light. Bathed in that bright warmth, you feel as though you too are brimming with a feeling of well-being and you haven't the slightest desire to flee. So, I stand before him thinking as if in a dream, "Wolf, we're not prowling around in the woods anymore now, but in gentleness. Still, you should know just what such gentleness is made of, shouldn't you? Whether it's simply what it appears to be and the forest is but a bunch of trees in which to take a walk. But in that case, where can the magnificent place in which the world unveils its violent truth — that place where you'll know me and I'll know you — be found?"

Finally, he says, "Let's go!"

Without using his hands to push away from his desk, where he had sat back down, his chair is scooted back, and he is already standing. But Mama, he couldn't dance with her. He hadn't tried, he hadn't stood up! But, as a matter of fact, when had that been?

I say, "I only meant later."

"What later?"

He puts on a falsely contrite look. I know him, don't let yourself be taken in by it. He's a lot smarter than you'd think — he's conjuring up an answer.

"Well, all right then," he says. "When you grow up to be as tall as I am."

My answer is ready right away. I come back at him, "And what about you, do you think you're big enough to meet . . ."

"What?"

Then I too hesitate, the word is right on the tip of my tongue. I'll say it . . . I won't say it . . . "a wolf," I say.

"Because you saw a wolf? And then what?"

I make terrifying eyes.

"I danced with him in the forest."

"So, you're just back from the forest."

"Yes."

"And what about the music?"

"What music?"

"To dance to! Was there a howling concert?"

"There was a howling concert and even a howling contest. I howled too . . ."

"And called for blood."

"Blood. Why blood?"

"I rather think that if, someday, I turn back into a wolf and go back to my forest, that's what I'd begin with."

"You're only half serious, Papa."

"There's not a father in the world who's more serious while talking to his daughter than I am talking to my daughter here and now."

"Oh, Papa! Is that lie really true?"

"No matter what she thinks and no matter what she says."

"Kyllä. Kyllä."

He sits back down in his chair and pulls himself up to the desk. He's either disappointed in his daughter or else I'm terribly mistaken.

"I promise I'll dance with you when I grow up."

"As long as it's not the waltz. Or the tango."

"The waltz or the tango? Who dances those anymore?"

Laughing this time, his eyes seem to be shining for something they fear they'll never find anywhere nearby. I hope with all my heart that they'll find it; it's not very likely.

"If you just have to wiggle around like they do today," he explains, "I'm game for that."

"You call that wiggling around?"

"Ah. What is it then?"

"Papa, you know."

In the end, his gaze has turned back in on itself. He's drawn in his light, but only to take on that velvety gentleness once again which fills, like in a dream, the eyes of certain animals. Papa has put on his wolf mask again, before I even noticed.

The Savage Night

I

They went outside, Beyhana following on Nédim's footsteps.

A kind of wound tore through the clarity of day, and the distinct presentiment of dusk pervaded the avenue.

Straight, vanishing lines. Barren geometry: the avenue; they kept on going. Occasionally, two or three figures would crop up in the distance, alive only in their miming the intent to advance or to retreat.

They would gesticulate and they would neither advance nor retreat. Silhouetted against the distant background of the avenue, gesticulating. Gesticulating, etched upon pure white fire. White. A fire that still shone wildly, as the impression of dusk had just barely gripped the air.

Without hurrying much, Nédim and Beyhana, or Bahi as Nédim rather preferred to call her, walked along side by side.

She was the first to turn, cast a glance at her brother. He acknowledged her look. They stepped up their pace.

Those figures out there, at the end of the avenue, still weren't advancing any more than they were retreating. Nédim and Bahi glanced at each other again. They both had the same smile on their faces, a smile that could have easily changed into giddy laughter. They refrained, turned their eyes away, and looked back down the street.

Slowly, the sky tinged with iodine, yet down at the end of the avenue it was still white-hot. As they passed, all was silent, the deep gardens and, barely visible, the snow-white villas caught in a tangle of lush green. The two young people had just slipped away from a villa very much like this.

The figures, down there, out of reach, were gesticulating without advancing or retreating farther.

Suddenly, from behind Bahi, from behind Nédim, a trolleybus came looming up and rumbled past them. "It actually grazed us," said Bahi indignantly. "It was snorting like a bull."

For an instant, the trolley blocked their view. As it was pulling up to the stop, they ran to catch it.

One person got off.

Hanging onto her brother's arm, Bahi was hopping up and down on her high heels, and Nédim stiffened, stiffened his arm to give her more support. The trolleybus, filled with rows of heads lined up by the windows, was off again, followed by a long groan as it pulled away.

Nédim had already leaped onto the rear platform. With his arm around her waist, he scooped up Bahi, who landed gasping by his side.

This time she didn't try to hold back the laughter that seized her. She directed it at him, incapable of pronouncing a word. Careening to one side, the vehicle threw them up against one another other in a curve. Bahi broke her fall with outstretched hands, very slender hands, that she left there, resting flat against her brother's chest.

Obstinate, rough jerks came in relentless succession, one after another. Unable to keep her balance and realizing that the jolts weren't over, she finally grabbed hold of her brother's wrist.

They laughed. Staring at each other, they encountered their own reflections and laughed some more. Two mirrors drawn to one another, probing one another.

Had they dressed themselves up — he in women's trappings, she in men's — they could have fooled anyone, they looked so much alike. Marveling both unconsciously and consciously at this duality, each believed they had an incontestable gift of ubiquity. Nédim breathed in Bahi's Chanel perfume. He didn't wear perfume, so that was the least he could do in return.

*

They were, and could be nothing but, children from an old Algiers family, the kind of natives from this city that have azure eyes. Nédim's eyes, like pure, scallop-shaped sapphires, when not momentarily dulled with a sudden glassiness, promised an equally luminous personality.

Hers, more elongated, making a slit that reached across the width of her face, took from the neighboring sea its deep, violet color and something suggestive of its continuous ebb and flow.

The brother and sister had also both been endowed with an abundant share of hair, cut short and curly (Nédim), hanging down loose, soft, and wavy (Bahi), and ranging from straw blond (Nédim) to a golden titian (Bahi).

Even their dissimilarities could have been exchanged. They could have exchanged everything. In the firmament of signs, they were Gemini, and Gemini they would remain.

*

Growing steeper and more sinuous, the streets began running downhill, pulling the trolleybus along, hurling it — mad, trumpeting elephant — into an uncontrollable stampede.

Nédim's eyes fell on Bahi's handbag.

"Nédim, don't worry," she murmured.

Bowing her head, she let two cascades of hair come tumbling down over both sides of her face. From beneath, mocking eyes peeped out. Her facial features tapered from the high cheekbones down to the chin, but with a telltale hint of seriousness in her voice, she added, trying to sound neutral, "This won't be the first time, will it?"

They left it at that.

Shaking out her thick mane, Bahi lifted her head and from then on just watched as doors, walls, gates, entrances, but fewer and fewer gardens whipped by, thrown behind them by the advancing trolley.

How can it be possible not to love her? Nédim was wondering. All of a

49

sudden, it had welled up in his throat, and it would have taken words to untangle his feelings. But there were no words for it. He would keep the pain to himself.

He watched as she contemplated the distant quarters of the city. He would keep the pain to himself. She had agreed once again to allow him to put her in danger. Words would be inappropriate.

Again, he glanced around at the people in the trolley. Vacant looks — they were resigned to their fate. It was plastered all over their faces: these people were just waiting to be led to the slaughter-house.

The trolley collected destinies, shed a few of them along the way, and, without tarrying, continued its descent. *On to the slaughter-house,* Nédim thought. *On to hell.*

*

And then, that familiar eclipse was sweeping over him. Without warning — that's the way it always happened. But as he went under, his senses would get sharper, would become charged with savagery. Sinking down into the darkest regions of madness, regions in which his resolve would nevertheless always find new strength.

Just like every time danger is near at hand. And now is the time. The danger ahead, not yet behind. The dragon, and you beat a retreat while moving toward it at the same time. Trying to calculate what afterwards would be like, and it would be whatever it would be. A trance, an interminable reflection, inconvenient when they come rushing over you but convenient when, at the gates of death, they become a refuge.

The voice speaking to itself in this way was suddenly startled to find that the trolley hadn't come to a standstill, that the vortex you were caught up in was endless, that everything was being swallowed up even faster than before, and that there wasn't . . . there wasn't . . .

You waited for the final wave, the one that buries everything in breaking, the tidal wave so immense it fills your vision. And then, that was all.

You closed your eyes. It didn't come.

The trolleybus kept on going. Nédim found himself back among the same anonymous passengers with their unchanged, destitute expressions — and Bahi. Bahi, whom he told himself he could never love more. Never. Never.

And afterwards, long afterwards, I will realize that this was the happiest moment of my life. Will I then be condemned to weeping in bitter regret? Is that the price I will have to pay? Will I be forced to admit that whatever comes to pass must also pass away?

The same blood that ran in his veins, the very same, nurtured Bahi's radiant beauty — that immutable, irrevocably beautiful presence.

Sweet love, I know not what favors I await from you. But for her, may the heavens lavish everything upon her! Compassion and anticipated nostalgia were gradually undermining Nédim.

The ripe, golden daylight was ablaze, yet it was also veiled in the shrouds of a martyr's agony. In the parks, certain trees — poplars, eucalyptus — were now but flaming torches. Out on the rim of the sea, as if aware of its coming death, the sun smoldered ever more ardently.

*

Nédim smiled. You could easily have thought that he was smiling at the sight of the city, which dissipated as it spread out. But no, his smile was directed at an inner vision.

His mother and father were standing nearby, yet at some distance from each other and seemed as if they were just about to say . . . he listened very closely: what was it? But a deep silence fell between him and them. At first he didn't suspect the silence of being quite so complete, and one would have sworn that the silence itself, forming a circle at the edge of which everything stopped, was going to speak. Nédim was still trying to say, *Mother, Father, what is it that you want to tell me?*

Neither of his old parents opened their mouths. He was standing there listening, full of hope. Were they going to make up their minds to speak? Then he finally had to admit they seemed to be there simply for the sake of being there, protected in that circle of silence.

Is it possible that you've already spoken and I didn't hear you?

He thought he saw them nodding their heads yes. But in what language had they spoken for him not to have understood them? Or else, though the words pronounced were familiar enough, had they faded away before reaching him?

Fundamentally, that was an impossible question to answer, and the scene that had sprung from nowhere dissolved and vanished.

Dragging along buildings, squares, statues, parks, gardens where exotic trees cropped up unpredictably amid the local vegetation stinted with stony dryness, the city reeled down like a whirling dervish toward the fleetingly glimpsed sea, the sea that was carefully gathering the last shimmerings of day upon her breast, perpetually rising and falling with a gentle rocking movement, and the dance would last long into the evening.

Maybe Mother and Father have discovered a few things about me. He wondered, then cut himself short. Nédim was deep in thought, he was in no hurry. *But what about Bahi? Uh-oh, if they ever have the slightest suspicion! The very slightest! Good god, the only reason they appeared just now was to find out, that's obvious. As usual, they proved themselves to be very discreet. Resigned? Resigned to the worst? They always have been and they haven't changed at all. Their honor had been slighted, but they'd always entertained the myth of lost grandeur, bleeding deep down in their souls but still dazzled by the mirage of olden splendors. Bereft of all self-respect, never raising their voices.*

He couldn't hold back. He burst out laughing.

Bahi, surprised, shot him a smile that fell just as quickly. Standing there before her was the body of an utter stranger — it deeply disturbed her. A stranger so wrapped up in his own solitude that he would forget you were even there. The horrid reality was like a slap in the face. She pitied him.

She pitied him, and yet an incomprehensible feeling of fear crept over her. What secret had changed Nédim into a stranger? Was it the same type of aberration that caused humans to develop from animals?

Up above the platform of the trolleybus, the sky reflected only peace and plenitude.

Bahi cursed inwardly. She wasn't one to let herself be tricked by this impostor.

"Should someone question the fact that I am just as much Nédim's brother and his shield as he is my sister and my shield, they would be making a big mistake. Nédim is me, and I am him."

Knowing that they were very privileged to be what they were re-assured Bahi. It occurred to her that Nédim would certainly make fun of her if she confessed her fantasies to him. She promised herself that she would tell him everything when the time came.

Darkness was beginning to gather out in the far corners of the sky, a darkness that did not appear to be simply vesperal.

Having regained confidence in herself, Bahi now watched the sky and the thickening darkness closely. Nédim still stood there, posing in the effigy of solitude. No jolt from the trolley justified it, but she grabbed hold of his shoulders with both hands. Now nothing but her handbag separated her from him — its strap had slipped down onto her wrist.

Just then, all of the vague anxiety hovering in the atmosphere of the trolleybus came rushing in on her. She realized that she was both totally infatuated and deluded by an absurd presumption and that it would lead to her own destruction. Being so utterly consumed with the desire to step through the mirror and its ripples and then step back through again drove her to secretly wish to live the forbidden dream. She didn't understand how or why she had ever come to have this dream, forgetting her resemblance to her brother, with that yawning cleft she carried in her loins exposing her to every imaginable trespass, forgetting that forgetfulness is the price one pays for life.

"Nédim, Nédim, and yet you're the one who has the solid body, the one who casts a shadow. And I, Nédim, I am that shadow, the empty shelter of your night."

Bahi, lost in thought, was the perfect image of light-hearted serenity, the perfect image of femininity, which she dutifully incarnated. But her gaze strayed, kept encountering the stony faces handed out to the passengers when they got on the trolleybus, kept imagining those sleepy, ashen eyes crying out, those pursed mouths screaming, crying, screaming out their fear of dying and their wish to kill.

The city, having splurged on all its finery, was now fading. Fading into the gray mist somewhere between the sky, the earth, and the sea, being transformed into glittering tinsel towers and palaces. The vision filled Nédim's eyes, yet he was no less aware of the nearness of soft skin stretched over a face and neck — skin, face, and neck of mist as well. He cursed impatiently: *When will the time come? When?*

With one hand still resting on his shoulder, Bahi gave him a little slap with the other. As though he had been startled from a faint, Nédim feigned a tic of the eyelids. He was still busy thinking: *These passenger dummies, soon, they too, they too will be offered up to the flames, reduced to smoke.*

"Only fifteen minutes to go," Bahi said.

She had checked her tiny watch and made that announcement. She even added, "Yes, almost."

Nédim shot such a direct look at her that it intimidated her.

She dug her fingers like claws into his shoulders. Facing her, her brother's eyes, twinkling with amusement, grew wider. At last she was back with her old Nédim again and not that other, that stranger who had disguised himself as her brother. She shuddered again.

In an abrupt tone of voice, she asked, "How's it going?"

"Oh, it's coming and going. And you?"

He flashed that smile which made you weak in the knees. She bit her lip.

It was silly, but she couldn't keep quiet. "Here we are. We have to get off."

"All right."

"My prayers will always be with him."

Braking, the trolleybus slammed forward with all of its weight, swung back to an upright position; the last people to have gotten on were the first to step out — among them, Nédim and Bahi.

II

They stared at each other. The simultaneous winks they exchanged sealed their separation. Nédim was already walking away. Brother and sister were now strangers.

Yet Bahi was following him, only six or seven yards behind.

A boy wending his way through the seven o'clock evening crowd, what could be more ordinary? But a girl observing him from a distance, watching his movements, a girl being careful not to lose sight of him and following him, what if we were there watching her, studying her little game ourselves?

Soon Nédim, with the girl following after him, passed the university. The time-honored building towered before them, noble twice over with its double stone stairways, but neither he nor she deigned to look at it — no more so, for that matter, than they would tomorrow when they would go up these very steps.

Continuing along their way, they were separated by the distance they had intentionally put between themselves, but an invisible thread still united them. Nédim was glad to have firm ground under his feet now, rather than the dancing floor of the trolleybus.

Gaining ground on the city, the twilight was tearing down one façade after another, replacing them with swift neon strokes, blinking, multicolored variations. However, the sulfurous, gaudy colors, the strings of blazing shop windows, the incandescent tramways, the bright car headlights that went slashing through the dark density of the crowd were not enough to fill the empty places left by the demolition.

Nor was the sudden rise in the level of noise — cries of evening newspaper vendors, musical vociferations, rising clamors, bellowing boats — enough to dam up the floodtide of silence that when obstructed on one side would come seeping out on the other.

But Algiers the courtesan, out on the town at last, could parade around in its gaudy lights.

*

Driven by his cold determination, Nédim would have stopped at nothing. Sure of himself, he struck into the throng where oblivious people were colliding blindly with one another, but he, guided by his lucidity, saw, already knew, what he would do in the time it took him to reach his objective — any second now.

Bahi was still following at a distance.

Around the General Post Office, the crowd grew thicker. You would have thought that the flood of people were seething up from the ground. Nédim had to push his way through. He inched forward, bolstered by the knowledge that Bahi was close behind. The stupidest thing he could do right then was turn around and glance over his shoulder, try and pick her out in the milling crowd.

Instead, he lifted his arm and looked at his watch. *Another four minutes to go,* he thought.

As they were being swept along in that tide, expressionless heads kept bobbing up out of the shadows and immediately sinking back down, but some, more beautiful and more grave in the night lights — women's heads with sparkling eyes — emerged, encircled in an aura of bronze, and seemed to be able to stay above the surface longer, more easily. Yet, in an ephemeral flash, they reluctantly disappeared as well.

We'll stick it out to the very end. To our own end, to our last drop of strength. That's what Nédim was telling himself and thinking they would soon have to prove it, fully aware of the extent to which he drew his strength from Bahi being there behind him. He had no doubts. *To the very end . . .* And then, there it was. Coolness began to waft in from the sea, the air got crisper. He waited. Not for long. Something brushed up against him. Bahi. As he was stepping back to let her pass, he felt the coldness of metal in his hand. He closed his fist over that coldness. Bahi was already gone. He caught sight of her, glancing quickly about herself as she went along, shimmying through the crowd. And then she disappeared. No one paid any attention to them. No one bothered about them at all.

Standing still as though he had forgotten something, he — Nédim — pretended to be gathering his thoughts. Bahi soon came back, and he noticed how natural she seemed, how self-controlled. They faced each other, this time in a rapid, furtive chassé-croisé. She refrained from looking at him, from even seeing him. She just murmured indistinctly, "Excuse me, sir."

"Excuse me."

Again contact with metal, cold in Nédim's right hand. He had what he wanted.

She passed by.

How could he not love her? With nerves painfully taught, one, two, three steps, she, already far away, was running but keeping herself in check. He walked. They had planned for her to turn into the adjacent street, and then it would be all over with, she should get out of the neighborhood. He was walking. The atmosphere seemed to be charged with a sort of — what? — a sort of necrosis, like a black dot that had gotten irreversibly tangled. Death. All this time it had been walking arm in arm with those who shared in being overly suspicious, overly hateful, overly blind to what was at stake. But it had all been going on for much too long. *Now nothing will be able to keep this particular story from starting back at the beginning and rewriting itself differently and in letters of blood.*

One step, two steps. Unconscious enumeration while he himself turned projectile, turned with arm cocked.

Three, four. This was the spot. Five. The first grenade unpinned and thrown into the brasserie. Six. The second. Explosion of the first. Six. Explosion of glass. Seven. Explosion of screams, of cries. Seven. The other explosion, and the brasserie was blasted out of the ground, and the street, the street shaken, ruined.

Eight, nine . . .

Wild, running, fleeing men and women flung forward. Some fell as though cut down and yet still tried to get back on their feet, then fell again, stopped moving. The storefronts, the entrances to buildings swallowing, swallowing people up.

In the end, the only people left were those lying on the ground, and everything around them was desolate — the sidewalk, the street. Desolate. The silence desolate. In the aftermath of its fury, the lightning had vomited up its silence, and it lasted, spread out — a white nothingness gripping the city, gripping its asphalt heart.

The brasserie, flaming, bloody mouth, began then to emit gasps, wheezing moans. Time had no more time to waste on that: it was silenced and the mute hell was draped in an unspeakable fluorescent glow.

Nédim stumbled away on shaky legs — one step, two steps, three steps. Unable to think past that, but at least able to think that he had opened the wrong door.

*

A lone shot cracked out mortifying the silence, which now quivered again, clamped down over it, and then closed up like a wound over a white-hot blade: that was all.

A long time passed, but when more shots were fired — this time from several different directions — there was no end to them. Bullets spitting out of arms of every caliber, bursts of fire building one upon the other, the deadly shower was widening out, taking over the neighborhood. Soon, the racket itself was shattered, pounded to bits by marching salvos of machine guns.

After that, all that could be heard were the machine guns. The other guns hadn't stopped firing, but only seemed to be letting out insignificant little coughs.

Interminably, the minutes drew out. Then a concert of sharp whistles pierced the air, a line of armored vehicles emerged and, following one another in close procession, came to a standstill in front of the devastated building. At first, stationed in firing position, they barred access to the ambulances with howling sirens, determined to slip between them.

At the same time, the crowd came rushing back in force, laying siege to the ruined brasserie; so many curious, hysterical people forcibly turned back, but not being contained, they threw themselves into a renewed assault on the hastily thrown up barricades and, like flies clinging to the flesh of a dead animal, they could not be driven away by further attempts.

There were, nevertheless, a few who left of their own accord, pistol in hand, shooting randomly through the streets, at housekeepers, at fruit and vegetable vendors, at street hawkers, demanding revenge with cries of "Death to the culprits! Death!"

Here and there, one would also encounter real ladies sobbing, leaning up against a wall with their hands over their faces.

Caught up from the very beginning in the reflux, the crowd of onlookers falling back, and, like them, pressed and jostled, Nédim had found himself on the opposite sidewalk, telling himself: *take advantage of it, make it over to the corner, where all you'll have to do is turn and leave the tumult behind.* Saying to himself: *and then melt into the labyrinth of the city, melt into the night.* A wild urge to run was twisting his insides; he controlled himself. At the corner, he turned. The street sloped downward. He realized at that moment that he was moving more rapidly than caution would advise. He reined himself in.

At the other end of the street, posted as sentry, stood a dark figure. At this paradoxical time, a paradoxical presence? Suspicious, Nédim slowed his pace even more. Instinct warned him that the night held nothing but paradoxical encounters. He cursed and, throwing caution to the wind, went forward to meet the figure.

Though the other person up in front of him didn't seem to be moving, they were drawing nearer all the time. Nédim kept walking along. The other continued moving up the street toward him. He took longer strides. Bahi fell into his arms.

In truth, he let himself fall against her. If he had not, he would simply have crumpled up — if she hadn't caught him, hadn't offered him her shoulder so that he could rest his head, which he could no longer hold up.

The young girl, who had stumbled under his weight but managed to stay on her feet, wanted to shriek out. Instead, she whispered, "Nédim, Nédim! What's wrong?"

"I don't know. Nothing, I think."

She made her voice be calm, almost natural, and asked again, "Nédim, you haven't been hurt, have you?"

He didn't answer.

At that, she didn't hesitate to lift his head with her two hands and examine him ferociously. He didn't say a word. His eyes were closed.

All Bahi could do was shudder and accept this new face. So this was the Nédim they were going to leave her? Even so, this kind of sight didn't weaken her resolve or rattle her. She began by grabbing one of her brother's arms and putting it around her shoulder; she wound his other arm about her waist, and held up in this way, Nédim didn't resist, he began walking.

III

It was welling up, reaching the small of his back. He wasn't in pain, no, but his legs were growing curiously numb as he walked along. They kept buckling up underneath of him.

Then he became aware that Bahi was carrying him more than he was holding himself up. *There's something wrong. Bahi is pulling some sort of dead donkey along. I'm a dead donkey.*

He knew she was there — that came before everything else. So he must be pulling with her. He was pulling, keeping his eyes trained on a dim light shimmering far away in the depths of the night: a star. Were they going toward it or was it coming to meet them? The bright twinkling eye was hope smiling down upon them. He pulled even harder. That way it wouldn't take so very long for them to reach one another, them and the star; that way they would have outrun everything that could have happened to them that night.

We will have outrun death — death which had seemed so real back there. Just a bad dream to tell each other about when we wake up. And to laugh about. Laugh about together, Bahi, and we'll dance too. You're as good a dancer as I am. The sun will rise on another beautiful day. Shine on, little star.

Good God! He heard himself cursing. He was pitching forward. Luckily he hadn't gone and knocked his head up against the pavement. But why did the damn cotton on the ground stick to the soles of your feet like that?

Ah yes, outrun death! Just as you outrun your own shadow.

Night was crumbling into a whirling, sooty snow. And yet, even against this backdrop, the guiding light of the star sparkled on.

Then Nédim knew for certain that it couldn't be a real one — a star, that is — the atmosphere around it was a deathly pale.

One foot in front of the other. One step, then two steps, then three. They'd have to go check it out. It was still waiting in the same place. Then they could be sure about it.

And there, right before his very eyes, it disappears. And right before his eyes, a ballerina, no further away, in exactly the same spot, suddenly materializes to take its place and then begins twirling through the vaulted night sky, filling up the four corners of space and casting her smile about in all directions too.

Stop! Let us get to you! He had cried out to her, and it should have made the night blanch. But nothing: the night unchanged, the silence in which the city was steeling itself unchanged, and his cry had been wasted, if in fact he had uttered it at all.

Once again, he peered out in front of himself and found only legions of shadows.

He murmured, "Bahi, please."

"Yes, Nédim," his sister answered, maintaining the tone of calm assurance in her voice.

"When will we get there?"

"Hold on. We'll be out of danger soon."

What danger was she talking about? That was just like her, good old Bahi, to joke like that. The possibility that they wouldn't make it to the dancing star — could that be the danger? What a good old friend!

"Once we get to that star," he began again.

"What star?"

"What star!?"

In the dazed city and the unbroken, improbable night, a new day began to pale.

No less improbably, in that new morning light, he glimpsed Bahi running at an incalculable distance from him. He watched her cavorting, flailing about, surrounded by a sea of flames. Mesmerized, straining to see, he teetered, steadying himself with one hand against the nearest wall.

It was more like a vast Luna Park in which great banks of lights glared with a ghastly furor over the deserted, stopped rides; that's where she was whirling from one pirouette to another, in the very center, the brightest part of the blaze.

Why hadn't she taken him along too? He would have liked to go with her. He would have struck out on his knees if he no longer had legs to walk on.

In that very instant, he felt a sudden heaviness spread through his legs.

Bahi was explaining: "We don't have to hurry so much any more. Nédim, we just have to keep walking. Walking at a normal pace."

He stiffened, gathered his strength. In a sign of assent, he closed his eyes and then he just needed to move one foot, lift it: he started moving forward again. With those steps, he came back to his senses, back to reality, the same reality, the same night that had already found them roaming around earlier. The same night that could conceal so much, hold so much in store for them — ruin, punishment, the fluke that would delay them on their walk — *and you are ashamed for her, ashamed of yourself, with this body that is dissolving as you walk along. A body? More like a ghost tied to your footsteps.*

    *

Inside the flaming display window of a clothes shop, a half-naked dummy is watching him approach. Nédim minimizes the dark distance separating him from it, and it opens, leaving only a pane of glass between them now. He finds himself face to face with Bahi.

Eyes bulging, the young man stares at the dummy, and the dummy sizes him up from within her chasm of light.

The nightmarish lighting drains Nédim of all feeling as those glassy eyes scrutinize him, and he wonders if he will be able to stand that piercing look for very long. Wouldn't the spectral apparition come crashing down against the polished glass as soon as he tore his eyes away and stopped propping it up?

And yet Bahi, at his side, is letting him lean against her shoulders, against her body. A series of ominous thoughts — slowly, they come back around to close up the circle. And what if this is what it were like to die?

Who is it that is pleading with him all of a sudden? Bahi? The dummy?

"Come on brother, just a little farther. Do you hear, Nédim? Just a little farther and we'll be safe. Do you hear? Safe!

Those words cooing in his ear on one side, and on the other, the mute doll displaying itself, exhibiting itself in its cold nudity, the lights shining brightly down on it from above, shining up at it from below, false angel in a fiery shrine, smiling at him and there was only the glass between them. The end. This is the end. Questions. There aren't anymore questions to ask yourself, there aren't anymore that are relevant. At this point the best thing he can do is concentrate on what will inevitably happen. Even before he can return the angel's smile, he will fall down, down. Nédim will fall down, flat on his face. And there he was, still trying to say — but what more can he say?

Chlorotic sounds start gurgling up. They're coming from him:

With such a secret smile,
His lips did slightly part
But darkness filled his eyes

Unrecognizable, incongruous, his quavering voice had sung those few lines and then languidly died out. He thinks: *The night must have shed some tears of blood at some point. But you can't really tell. You can't see a thing.*

Whatever had been singing, that was the only thing that could have also wept. And he finds Bahi next to him, plastered against him, come back from out there where she had been roaming, whirling about and saying, bleary-eyed and smiling at the same time, tear streaks running down her cheeks, "You were singing, brother. I think I know that tune. It was, how can I say it . . ."

She wraps her arms around him, hugs him tightly. The boy's head falls back down onto her shoulder. She strokes his neck, runs her fingers through his hair, and questions him in a tender, anxious voice, "I know that tune. Who sings that?"

He hadn't fallen down. He's not going to fall down. Hoarsely, he admits, "I'm . . . I've been hit."

Bahi's cry explodes, "Baby!"

Her cry is muffled as she hugs Nédim tighter to her breast, rocking him.

He struggles to get free, gasping, "I've been hit . . . hit. Take it and go!"

"What should I take, Nédim?"

She's speaking right into his ear, and he, panting: "The gun. In my jacket pocket. Take it. Go. Run. Don't worry, I'll make it."

"Never."

He begs her, "Take it and go."

"Never."

His strength is dwindling; he tries to argue with her, "You shouldn't worry about me, pal. Really!"

"Never, Nédim. Never."

How would he ever make this stubborn mule change her mind?

"Listen," he begins again, then decides not to go on.

He thinks, *She's struggling against just as much exhaustion, just as much despair as I am.*

Without letting go of him, Bahi leans back slightly, stares at him. The street is so dimly lit that the young girl can barely make out her brother's features and even less decipher what she would like to see in that face. But it doesn't discourage her. In a whisper, she coaxes him, "Keep on going, my little Nédim. Keep leaning on me, and let's walk. You can do that. You'll see, everything will be fine. No, leave your arm around my shoulder. Or is it too tiring?"

He shakes his head no.

"Now, walk," she says. "People will think we're lovers."

IV

They went off into the night.

The city that had at first slowly tightened its coils around them was now widening out. The streets rolled on, almost deserted, almost candid. A couple of sweethearts were taking their time on their way home, a scenario you couldn't invent and, above all, that didn't stand out but actually fit right in with the surroundings.

A low rumble — the storm of madness behind them hadn't blown over yet — regularly punctuated with the sound of shots ringing out, but that didn't mean much anymore.

Cars came roaring up and passed. Army jeeps, some of them. Far away, the octopus stretched out its tentacles. Hadn't Nédim and Bahi succeeded in putting enough distance between it and them? Apparently, it had only given them a bit of a head start, that's all.

From one of the vehicles, jokes came hurling through the night at them. They were paratroopers. Bahi didn't pay any attention. The only thing on her mind was holding Nédim up. Every now and again, glancing up at him quickly, she would try to get a look at his face to make sure he was all right. From what she could make out, her brother, eyes half shut, with his head lolling about from side to side, could only concentrate on the number of steps they were taking. In truth, he was totally absent. He was walking, but was completely oblivious — oblivious to himself, to the world.

Their only hope of salvation, Bahi believed, was in this walking. Just keep moving forward, keep going. Keep moving forward, keep going, not stopping for anything. Also, walking was the only way she would be able to figure out which way to go — figure out a way to get out of this mess and get Nédim out too.

Then she began shaking each foot, trying to throw off of her pumps. She was fed up with them. The high heels had almost made her sprain her ankle several times. Contact with the cool ground was a relief.

They came out into a crossroads. Without hesitating, she turned left. She was nearly carrying her brother.

Exhausted now, she couldn't go any farther and decided it was best to prop Nédim up against the front of a house. She took the opportunity, using both of her hands, to wipe away the sweat she could see running down his face, his forehead, his temples, to smooth down his hair while she was at it, and to murmur all the loving words she could think of in his ear.

She was giving herself time to catch her breath and hoping that Nédim would also get a hold of himself and start out again with a surer foot. The whole time, she never let her guard down for a second. Army cars, police cars, or private cars, which were just as dangerous, might suddenly appear out of thin air and arrest them.

Ready to bolt at the slightest sign of danger, she stood there alert. Then, not being able to stand it any longer, she dragged her brother on. They went across. A dark, protective street, running downhill to the harbor, welcomed them. Instinct convinced the young girl that this street was the gateway to freedom. Bahi felt that she had to reach the harbor, the wharves. They would be safe there. She promised herself they would get there. She made it her personal responsibility.

Like a runner who pushes onward only through sheer will-power, Nédim was heaving and panting.

"Why don't you sing that song again, the one you started a little while ago?" his sister suggested. "You don't have to sing very loud.

Just like you were before. Will you, please? I think I'll be able to remember the rest of it."

She could recall that the first lines went: *With such a secret smile, his lips did slightly part* . . . Now what jeep would ever dare take this street, with its long flights of stairs and these interminable, steep grades? First there's the music, but when it gets to the end, the song begins. And at the end of the song — when it discovers it is limited? — the words are left bare. And at the end of the words — when the source is run dry? — there is, once again, the song. Or the scream. And the music? The music . . . Would a jeep ever venture down here, a jeep would go tumbling head over heels, all the way down to the bottom. That was the way in which thoughts kept running around in Bahi's mind, while silence had become Nédim's viaticum. Nédim, for whom the silence was a heavier weight to bear than his weakness. Who, in parting his lips, could manage to emit only rattling, gasping sounds. He hadn't sung again, he would not sing again. Silence had become his song.

Step by step, holding him up, Bahi made her way over in that direction, toward those stairs. They would soon be there. One more test for her brother. "If only the streets," Bahi thought, "had the faculty of intorsion, they could simply curl up, and it would be so simple for them to conceal us. The dogs would never be able to track us down then. But they just run on in these cursed straight lines, dooming the hunted!"

Suddenly, the long snake of a patrol slithered warily out of the night. It had been quite some time since Bahi had felt so safe. The only precaution she took was to huddle up in the doorway of a building, pulling Nédim in after her. Leaning up against the door that not a prayer in heaven could open, she waited for the armed group to march by. They were already going past the doorway, machine guns leveled. She grabbed Nédim's head, covered it with her own, and in a hushed voice, ordered him: "Look at me, do you hear? Open your eyes, kiss me."

She placed her mouth upon the boy's listless lips; Nédim's eyelids fluttered then gave way to the most horribly distant look imaginable. Bahi remembered the other words of the love song: *But darkness filled his eyes . . .* He had started singing that song spontaneously, as if he were delirious. Disturbed by these thoughts, the young woman had not felt it coming before, but now the faint pressure of Nédim's lips was upon hers.

"Hem!" Coughed the first soldier in the file as he passed.

The others imitated him: "Hem! Hem!"

They disappeared down the deep, narrow street. The air suddenly seemed lighter.

"It's lucky they didn't hear the bass drum pounding in my chest." While Bahi was still trying to pull herself together, huddling in the entrance of that building with her brother, a window banged open on one of the upper floors.

Predictably, a voice boomed out: "Hey, you lovebirds! You've really got the nerve! This is a great time for necking! Do you have any idea what's been going on? But then you couldn't care less, could you? Hurry up and get the hell out of here now!"

Lovers: they had been given confirmation from above, Bahi thought. It hadn't been a bad idea at all. From then on, Bahi would see everything as a sign, an omen.

Nevertheless, she was on the verge of begging for a reprieve, but instead, she responded as if to herself: Yes, get the hell out of here, that's all we're asking for.

With Nédim in her arms, she struck out again into that night possessed with the Devil and his hosts, and soon, one step at a time, they somehow made it down the large flight of stairs.

Bahi had to match her pace to her brother's stumbling steps. She was taking him down to the harbor, but she felt so good in her stocking feet that she could have just kept on going, all the way to the end of the world. And yet she knew the harbor was near and thought she had been truly inspired to think of going there. She was congratulating herself as though she had actually invented the place. What else could they do? Go back home? How could they even dream of it? They would have had to go back to the center of town, get on a trolleybus. With Nédim in this shape? It'd be simpler just to give themselves up to the military police. Take a taxi? No, that was hardly a better solution.

    *

The wharves, the dark, secret places, the warehouses, the piles of freight, the crates, the cranes, the last hope of refuge, the harbor could only be deserted at this hour. They had to get there. Now it was really becoming urgent. Now Nédim was but a lifeless rag. Bahi was surprised she had the strength to haul him around and not have him crumple up at each step, simply lie down on the ground and not get up again.

  "Come on, Nédim, just give it one last effort."

  She never lost faith in him. She was prepared to stand by and defend him, no matter what happened.

  "Let's walk a little farther, and we'll be there."

  She received only a weak sigh in answer. The young woman tensed her muscles, dragged him in, and he came.

  Despite the taste of tears in her mouth, she started out with him again. She had been infected by the sickness of the hot, feverish body in her arms and she too was burning up. But she refused to let herself take another rest.

  They went down between curtains of thick shadows that long blades of light tore through intermittently, sank down into fathomless chasms that Bahi's exhausted eyes tried to probe. Her heart was beating so fast she thought it would burst, banging around in her chest, making her forget about the harbor awaiting them.

  Damned harbor! She suddenly pulled on Nédim harder than she had meant to, and, at the thought that she had ill-treated him, something small sobbed within her.

    *

The harbor was there.

  When she realized that, they had already started in to the ghostly place — disconnected from the world — which seemed to have drifted up and materialized just for the two of them.

The lapping of sleepy, invisible water echoed to itself from a distance. A light mist still smelling of fish, of fuel oil, of tar rising from the docks laid an intangible, damp hand on Bahi's face. As if in order to enter this place one must be recognized. Here and there, lampposts shed their pallid, sick light in vain. Though they could not penetrate the darkness, they were, or at least the young woman saw them to be, bearers of good tidings, and their fitful flickering was like friendly winks of the eye.

Supporting Nédim under the arms, she finally lowered him gently to the ground and settled down next to him, with her back up against what she imagined to be a bin. She stretched out her heavy, leaden legs and lifted her head to take a deep breath. She would have prayed if she'd known how. She felt something that rather resembled regret. Her forehead, her eyelids, her eyeballs underneath, all felt as though they were cast in lead.

Nédim was still sitting there exactly as she had left him, his head hanging apathetically upon his chest, not moving a muscle: a dark shape that seemed to grow less distinct every time she glanced in his direction. She was tormented with the thought that the real Nédim had been separated from his body by some terribly mysterious process — if that were the case, what sort of world was he off to? And what if it wasn't really her brother sitting beside her but someone else — who could it be? Yet describing it in that way still cannot adequately express how she felt, how you would feel having something like that touching you — that ashen, empty hull — and having to decide what to do with it.

As Bahi contemplated the string of glimmering lights following the infinite curve of the bay in an attempt to span the empty night, all kinds of thoughts assailed her. Without really being aware of it, she was trying to figure something out about the bright landmarks; she wasn't exactly sure what. Then suddenly, it struck her: the position of a house, a villa, out there hovering over the sea in that white plume of mist. She felt a lump rise in her throat. Their house.

Abruptly, huge wings of damp fog unfolded and beat down upon them. Bahi shuddered, overcome with a feeling of solitude and of imminent danger.

She rose to her feet, pulled Nédim up, and slipped into the night that, strangely enough, seemed to be as wide-open as it was locked up, that in its facelessness hid them, but also hid those who pursued them, hid that abomination which it is impossible to fend off. Bahi still hadn't discovered the secret place where, perhaps, no one would come to rout them out.

With Nédim in her arms, she walked along the railroad tracks that ran out from the city, casting threads of steel into the harbor. Deep in the rear of the docks just then, she happened to catch sight of a spot where she thought they might be safe. They'd hole up in there until things calmed down and, with some luck, maybe they would get out of this alive.

The ground suddenly trembled under their feet: with a screeching roar, flashing and fuming, a leviathan-train shook the night on all sides, whipping them with its wind, and then passed, leaving everything breathless, vibrating for an instant, the harbor roused from its lethargy, Bahi with her heart pounding wildly, and her brother still leaning up against her.

After she dragged Nédim along for another twenty feet or so, the blinding beam of light from a projector lit up the young woman. Exorbitant, the eye of the cyclops cast about, obliterating the dismal panorama of derricks, overhead cranes, ships at anchor silhouetted against the sky, then mercilessly exposing, down below, the darker horizon of the wharves and their buildings. It was sweeping the night into big piles and closing all the exits.

Nédim: *one step, and then one step, walking like this will lead me back to myself. I'll end up finding myself again, finding the beast that is eating away at me, the beast that is mad with love. It's already eaten my eyes away, eaten my brain away, eaten my heart away. It will end up taking me over completely. It will*

The Savage Night

become one with me, and we'll find ourselves under a black snow that will bury us
before giving it all up to white innocence. I can see ... No, I can't see a thing.

The bolt of savage light that was incinerating the emptiness it
had created finally spoke. Bahi heard the voice decree stonily: "Papers!"

V

Ziza, a torpedo on legs, bursts into the room but, struck by the profound silence she is desecrating, stops, petrified. It takes her no
longer than this shocked moment to sense the presence of the
woman sitting by a window in the dim light, looking out on a
luxuriant garden that the little girl, following her eyes, can barely
see from where she stands, fascinated — with what? Ziza remains
standing there until her eyes can once again frame the far end of the
room, the form of the woman against that background, and also
the window etched there with its vanishing lines; then she runs
and throws herself on that woman, neither old nor young (but that
doesn't matter to Ziza) who still has her eyes fixed on the garden.

The woman wraps one arm around her, and Ziza, without trying
to free herself or even to lift her head, asks, "Aunt Bahi, why don't
you come and sit with us?"

Pinned down as she is, she stretches out one hand and points to
where she means — somewhere in the other part of the house.

"You're always sitting here by yourself. Do you prefer being
alone?"

The answer is long in coming. Then finally, it comes.

"I'm an old lady, and it isn't right for old ladies to impose their
company on others, on young people."

A slow voice, very distant as it rises, pronouncing one word, then
another, entirely detached from the preceding one.

The little girl protests, "You're not old! You're not old!"

She's almost on the brink of tears. She goes on, "And anyway,
you're not really a lady! You never married! Aunt Bahi, why didn't
you ever marry?"

Once again, the answer takes time to come, surely not time to reflect, but time which is simply suspended.

"The man I loved went far away . . ."

"And you're waiting for him to come back?"

The woman acquiesces with a barely perceptible nod of her head. Her gaze seems to have been definitively lost in contemplation of the garden.

"And you just think about him all the time."

In saying this, had Ziza understood that her question was not really a question and that there was no answer to her question? Lifting her eyes, she studies, for no particular reason, those other eyes of a violet-blue, so strikingly like the color of the sea. No wave would ever wish to trouble such a clear, placid sea.

The Merry Misfit

I

He's just standing there thinking, as if he were faced with a terrible predicament, with his billfold cradled in his hand and his fingers curling lightly over the black leather. He seems very reluctant to open it.

Suddenly, he makes up his mind. No matter what, and regardless of how dire the consequences, he's come to a decision. He surely hadn't taken his billfold out of his pocket for no reason. He flips it open. It is the kind that unfolds like a stenographer's notebook rather than a book. On the inside of the upper flap are two slots, open on one end, sewn closed on the other. He (the man) slips two fingers into the larger one, finds a photograph, and pulls it out into the light. It's a small, color close-up of himself. Himself, just as he is now, or almost — the thick mask with its salient features. He still hasn't gotten used to that mask and those traits — he hates to think of them as his own. How does he feel looking at them? It seems as if, way down underneath, there is a deep cavern — the kind of cavern in which, every now and again, the hollow plunk of a tear-shaped drop of water echoes out.

Hastily, he returns the photograph to its place. In the next slot he finds another one, also a close-up, also in color, also of him, but dating back at least fifteen years. He doesn't linger over it — it doesn't resemble him at all any more. It too is quickly slipped back into its compartment from which he then draws an expense account. Not surprisingly, he's familiar with the handwriting — the expenditures and the sum of money changed during a trip to Sweden had been jotted down in his own hand. The piece of paper also goes back where it came from, near the photo. Then he notices, in the same compartment, a narrow scrap of paper scribbled with a series of numbers: 40 19 18 09. A telephone number. Whose was it? The man no longer has the slightest recollection, makes no effort to remember; he watches the narrow slot close over the paper.

Sprawling out lazily between the two banks, the Seine seems to be quivering with languid pleasure. Would it really be surprising if the light twinkling sleepily from its surface on this bright afternoon brought back flashes of a lost dream?

For an instant the man drifts, lost in contemplation of the river, then with a start returns to inspecting the billfold laying open in his hand. He flips over a second flap. On the other side is a small plastic window. The man fishes out his ID card. No need for that anymore. He takes out still another paper: his voter registration card. No need for that anymore. A credit card. No more credit, no more need for that. He draws one last card from the billfold — his blood type — examines it: Rh: *A positive*. He wonders what the letters mean. Little matter, he doesn't need to know anymore.

He scoops them all into a pile and stuffs it back under the little window, for once his identity card is not first in place under the plastic covering. His pink driver's license is neatly tucked away into a folding plastic sheath as well. The man opens it out; the black and white photograph stapled to the first fold leaps out at him. Still another snapshot, a three-quarter view this time, glaring at him. He returns its fixed stare. He doesn't recognize himself in this shot either, doesn't recognize himself in the young, morosely serious face, even though it is the very face that by some incomprehensibly ironic or absurd twist of fate authenticates the official document issued in his name.

His fingers slip from the edge of the opened driver's license, and it automatically folds back up to its original size. No need for that anymore. The car had been sold. He hadn't even obtained half the price it was worth — it was a fairly new car. The whole sum had gone to paying off a few of his debts.

The man needs to lift up the driver's license in order to be able examine the contents of the other transparent plastic sheaths underneath of it. The first one is empty; however, through it, he can see the photograph inserted in the second one. Without removing it from its protective covering, the man contemplates it. A two-inch-square, full-length picture of a couple of young girls posing. One of them, the slightly taller girl, has her arm thrown over the other's shoulders. Neither of them can be more than six years of age. The camera happened to catch them laughing, and what an extraordinary laugh it is! The girl whose arm is draped around her companion has an idiotic, gaping grin on her face, whereas the other, tempted to let herself go yet not quite daring to, is puckering her lips up and simply flashing a prim little smile. The man recalls having found that old-maidish expression unpleasant in the past. Suddenly today, something new has just dawned on him. She was probably missing some teeth and didn't want it to show. But that wasn't the only reason the child was trying to hold back her laughter. One hand was also opened wide and pressing against her lower abdomen.

He was to marry her later on, and that little girl would forever remain a stranger to him, an enigma. She had given him the photo shortly before they were married. Had she told him anything about her childhood friend? He couldn't recall.

In the same plastic sleeve, but on the back side, were other photographs — two of them, and this time they were of the same breathtakingly beautiful woman. To explain that in both snapshots her head is slightly tilted back and so seems to offer up her eyes like two brimming cupfuls of light, to explain that those eyes hold a profound and distant mystery while at the same time being so marvelously open to the exterior world, to explain what her smile is like, to explain this — that and a thousand other things — could never even begin to explain her magical charm, her irresistible appeal. That young kid, with the old-maid smile plastered on her face, is her.

One of the two pictures has been cut into an oval shape for a locket, but the other, in standard format, is a half-length portrait of the woman leaning with her forearms on a table or a desk. In both her head has the same relaxed tilt, and the face, the same more or less ecstatic smile. There isn't a single photo of her in which that smile isn't shedding an aura of light about her face.

He barely even glances at these photographs before going on to the third sheath. It also contains a snapshot of a woman. The picture is taken from the base of the woman's throat down to her waist — the head is not included. The indiscreet eye is immediately drawn to the whiteness of a breast protruding from the low neckline of a corsage and joined to a baby's mouth. The only thing the man considers, in fact, are the three necklaces and a pendant that hang around the woman's neck — gifts from him. He turns the sheath.

On the other side of the picture is a membership card — expired — to a tennis club. That's the end of everything. The back flap of leather shows only a dark, empty window, exactly symmetrical to the one on the front flap.

No, that isn't where everything ends. There's still the secret compartment for holding paper money that runs the whole length of the billfold, forming its outer skin. The man spreads it open, revealing some bank notes — six of them. He thumbs through them and quickly transfers the money to one of his pockets. He notices still another card, hidden between the bills. Flicking it out with one finger, he discovers that it's his social security card and stuffs it back into the wallet. No need for that anymore. Then, closing the billfold again, he leans back right where he is sitting, arches his back, winds his arm up, and flings it out toward the Seine.

The object describes a wide arch, then drops into the water. The splash one might have expected does not come, and there are no ripples on the surface of the water either.

A blissful expression illuminates the man's face. He continues to pat his chest searchingly with both hands, feels a bump through the material of his jacket, and guesses: his address book. He extracts it from one of his inside breast pockets and tosses it out into the river along with the billfold. Sometimes a simple gesture can suddenly make you see the light. But what kind of gesture? And who could ever have told you about it?

The Seine, its banks, the oldest part of the city pushing out its bristling snout, shaggy with trees over on the right, and the footbridge on the left, not far off, with its endless parade of two-legged ants, the air, the sky, and suddenly something quite subtle, almost ethereal: "But life must also admit its faults and ask forgiveness, if that's possible." The man thinks it over for a minute and adds, "It's not enough for life to simply be whatever happens to you."

All the same, sitting there on the bench with his jacket unbuttoned, his legs spread out in front of him, his arms stretched along either side of the backrest, he feels as if he at least fills up the entire bench, if not the entire bank of the river. He remains in that attitude of total abandonment, lulled by the hum of the traffic.

Suddenly, his feet come up underneath of him, the man stands up straight and tall, he walks away. He does not head back up in the direction of town but rather goes for a stroll along the strip of the embankment reserved for pedestrians.

Soon he passes under the arch of Pont-Neuf and immediately afterwards having reached the end of the promenade, turns to walk back.

He returns to the bench but goes past it without even stopping, ambles along by the river for a time — he doesn't care how long — and finally, coming to the other end, his little stroll is cut short again. He turns around for the second time. How is it possible to think clearly under these circumstances? There are fences and barriers everywhere.

Coming back to the bench, he finds it is now occupied. A young couple sits intertwined right in the middle of it. The man walks up and sits down at one end anyway. Just as he is taking a seat, the two lovebirds get up and leave. He watches them walking away. "I scared them off."

Had he ever known what the meaning of respect for other people was? Never, he admits. "And just who do you think you are now, anyway? Still some kind of a hot shot?" He's sitting there alone now, and he hears himself asking the question again: "And just who do you think you are now, anyway? Still some kind of a hot shot?" He slides his buttocks over to the middle of the bench. He is completely alone. That's what he had wanted wasn't it? Above all, he wants to be spared hearing that phrase echoing over and over again: "And just who do you think you are now, anyway? Still some kind of a hot shot?"

He chuckles — he has nothing more to hide: "The truth comes out when the going gets rough. Swearing that they may tear out your tongue when there is nothing else left to say." And he adds: "The truth comes out when it rears its horrid head."

He's not alone. His personal demon is sitting quietly beside him. The man ignores it. The sound of the traffic is so loud he feels as if it is grinding him up, crushing him.

Night falls and brings with it the blooming of a myriad of luminous flowers on the Seine. He hasn't budged from his place on the bench. He is lost in such deep contemplation of the shimmering flowers he nearly passes out, becomes the underwater bed of a silent river straining to hear the rumble coming from above.

The night grows thicker, and the flowers of light still haven't closed. The decor hasn't changed either. Nothing has changed. It's just that instead of bobbing around in the same spot all of these luminous blossoms seem to be floating swiftly downstream in a neat line. Also, there's not a soul to be found on the deserted banks of the river, no one but a man who believes the river has cleansed him of his name and re-baptized him with a new one, which he is waiting to learn. And if the humming noise with which the city seems to fill the darkness is right on his heels, he might be justified in thinking that his ears are ringing due to his age. The fact is, there are fewer and fewer cars. Fewer and fewer until, over the insistent, low murmur, only a faint, animal purring sound can be heard.

He spent the night on that bench. The biting chill in the air toward early morning has faded from his memory since the sun has come up. Standing, he takes particular pleasure in stretching himself repeatedly, yawning to his heart's content. His limbs feel somewhat stiff and his ribs are sore from the hard, wooden bench, but he himself is more rested than if he'd slept in his own bed. He feels as courageous as a lion. He becomes aware of a growing sense of pride.

Then he leaves the Seine and goes off to join the stream of humans that have already started their day at a run. "It's like a high-speed treasure hunt that is actually just a race, simply for the sake of having a race." The automobiles have also begun their wild, inexorable rounds.

At a light that is taking too long to turn red and dam up the flow of traffic, he just bides his time patiently. He's got nothing to lose from waiting. And so he waits. It occurs to him that he had been truly inspired to have kept the cash before throwing everything else into the river. One of his high school courses comes to mind: the gratuitous act. Debates with his fellow students, all those memories, all that crap that the teachers used to feed them. And they, the promising young men, avidly soaking it all up, conscientiously learning their lesson: how to speak without really saying anything. A gratuitous act if there ever was one.

Abruptly, the street is clear. He walks across and goes into a café almost directly opposite the traffic light.

II

He only decides to come out of the toilet stall in order to try and wash up using the little gushes of water that the faucet sparingly dispenses with each press of the knob. But what a wonderful place for thinking things through!

As he is drying himself off with a paper towel, the mirror calls his attention to the outgrowth of beard on his face and the extent to which the sandy stubble sprinkled over his cheeks has spread. He quickly notes, nevertheless, that a blonde's beard is much less intimidating than that of someone with a darker complexion. His will grow to be quite bushy. He can already imagine those indifferent, blue eyes peering out blankly from amid the thick whiskers. This whole place exudes a light scent of lavender detergent. It is as clean as it is quiet. Not a sound.

Back in the café, before taking a seat, he orders a sandwich to go along with his coffee. Since he is the sole patron at this early hour, the service is prompt. And so, he eats his breakfast at the same time as his dinner from the night before.

The doorframe looks exactly like a giant television screen. It creates the same type of illusion. Cars race by, vanishing eerily off to one side before suddenly lunging back with a crazed vengeance from the other, endlessly roaring after one another in a game of hot pursuit.

It's no wonder that a faint smell of exhaust fumes mingles with the acrid stench of stale wine, beer, and tobacco, which are the types of odors one might expect to find in this kind of place.

While the man is eating, drinking, and straining with all of his senses to tune into the dull vibration that is emanating from the floor, the walls, and the air, two dark shapes appear in the doorway. One begins by inviting the other to go in first. The invitation is declined on both sides, which causes both to start out together, jostling one another as they pass through the door, and reveal at last their antediluvian appearance: tall characters on long, spindly legs upon which they move about rhythmically, quite overdressed for the season. They hadn't interrupted their conversation once, not even when they reached the bar and called to the waiter without bothering to make sure that he was listening to them or even that he was at his post back there with the coffee machine, the beer tap, and the display of multicolored bottles:

"I'll have a glass of regular white wine."

"Same for me."

Both of their voices are gravelly. They clear their throats every now and again, but that is the only breather they allow themselves.

"We'll never know for sure, I tell you."

"We'll never know?"

"Never."

"Still, we should try and find out."

"If it's in any way possible! Yes, if it's possible!"

"But you do agree, it's our duty to try."

"Our duty, our duty. If it's in any way possible!"

"If it's in any way possible? And what if that's all we can do?"

"All we can do? Damned right!"

"Damned right . . ."

"Yes, damned right!"

Then, as if in silent agreement, without even looking at their glasses, they both reach out and take them in their knotted hands.

*

The man comes out into Place Saint-Michel. He has no particular plans in mind. Unable to decide which way to turn, he wonders whatever brought him there. He hasn't set foot in the Latin Quarter for ages, ever since that public conspiracy of hope that erupted in May of '68. Even he had believed in it.

He hesitates, then walks up Boulevard Saint-Michel. A tank truck is still in the process of spraying a swift stream of water into the gutter that the street sweepers are whisking along in rhythm. Up and down the long street, the countless sun-splashed leaves of plane-trees are set to quivering: Paris is having its morning shower. There's an invigorating atmosphere of freshness and well-being. The man would almost be taken in by it, almost accept it at face value, if he didn't feel as if he were moving backward in time, toward the days of his youth, and suddenly begin to feel increasingly nauseous.

Gradually, his queasiness subsides. The boulevard reveals what it has now become: a series of fashion boutiques. He might, at the very least, have caught a glimpse of himself in the mirrors of the ever-present beer parlors he is passing one by one if they too hadn't, in their own way — heaped with outrageous, flashy trappings — demeaned themselves in the name of keeping a youthful face.

"Life brings only suffering to all living things."

He beats a hasty retreat.

The man soon gets back to the intersection and crosses Boulevard Saint-Germain again, but this time he turns up Rue de la Harpe and walks toward Saint-Séverin. Things have changed there too. The exoticism of the *almées* has rubbed off on almost every corner dive. Palaces from *The Thousand and One Nights* line the street. What kind of people go there? It's too early in the day to tell. He wanders around a bit in the narrow, winding alleyways, then takes a short-cut through Rue Saint-Jacques, walks past Saint-Julien-le-Pauvre, and comes out on the embankments lining the riverside.

The city is but a thin screen upon which shadows pass. All along the parapets of the Seine, the bouquinistes are laboriously opening their oblong wooden stands.

Continuing the even stride that he has now grown used to, he reaches Ile Saint-Louis and tromps around on it without even thinking twice. To his mind, the same antiquated collections exist everywhere. He is quite familiar with this planet. He has traveled it from New York to Tokyo, from Cairo to Hong Kong, from Paris to Moscow by way of Helsinki, from London to Los Angeles.

Finding himself in the neighborhood of Saint-Paul, he becomes completely disoriented. Had he somehow landed on another planet? He can no longer put his finger on that unique and universal world he was so accustomed to leaving off in one part of the globe only to run into the same thing elsewhere — identical in every way, universal in every way, familiar in every way. On foot, a half hour stroll later, he has the feeling of being someplace that doesn't really exist. On foot, a half hour stroll later, he is immersed in a central Europe that is exactly as he imagines it — that is, enthralled with the Orient, exactly as he imagines it too. He is a clandestine emigrant, lost in this place, which is something between a ghetto and a medina, this place that without really setting itself apart would nonetheless be ashamed to just blend in.

A whirlwind of seething humanity giving off a dark animal odor

— more of a foreigner here than he had ever been in Tokyo, New York, or Moscow, he is buffeted in its tides. Some of the inhabitants parade around in huge black hats, out of which flow equally black beards. Taciturn keepers of the tabernacle, they glide easily through the knotting crowd. As for the others . . . Well, they all seem to have agreed to strike out on a quest of some sort, but of what sort exactly? They are searching, that's all. Who knows, perhaps they're trying to find the country that pins them in on all sides while at the same time shutting them out on all sides. They are seeking an answer in this street bazaar, this tumult punctuated by the impetuous cries of street hawkers, and they are terribly insistent because it is an absolute necessity.

Fruits, vegetables, meat, fish, used objects, secondhand clothes, five-and-dime articles, shops filled to the very brim spill out onto the sidewalks, into the garbage-strewn street, where with each step one is in danger of slipping and finding oneself flat on one's face while vendors call out from stall to stall at the top of their lungs to passersby, causing the hubbub to boil up, swell, intensify to the point that it seems to be coming from a veritable Tower of Babel that has finally been raised to the very heights and crowned in this rumor as if in heavenly song — a song which has apparently even reached some ears in the remotest of places since it is plain that the crowd is composed of wretches from all corners of the earth.

Down in that milling throng, there is, however, one person who, determined to make his way through the immense press of people by judiciously applying the force of his elbows, knees, and shoulders, does not realize that someone has been pulling at the tail of his jacket for several minutes.

The discreet tugs finally become so insistent that he turns around. A young boy of around ten energetically slips a scrap of paper into his hand. Having delivered the missive, the dark-skinned lad stands barring his way and staring at him with the determined eyes of a mountain goat.

The man looks down at his open hand and the square of paper

folded in its center without appearing to understand. Then, still perplexed, he examines the child. And the child, surprised by this show of impotence, attempts to explain using sign-language. The man seems to be primarily interested in observing the eloquent fingers and the gangly youth who is so expert with them: thread-bare trousers, faded tee-shirt, thin without being sickly, a frantic will to live reflected in those deep, dark eyes. The boy soon ceases his antics.

Then he (the man) unfolds the paper and deciphers the scrawl: "I am a Romanian Refugee. I am an Orphan. I have no Money. I'm Hungry."

But just as his hand nears his pocket, a voice, coming from the same general direction as the boy had, roars out from behind a veg-etable stand: "You'd better be getting along now, you dirty little thief! He's always hanging around here and stealing stuff. I caught him red-handed! Watch out for your wallet! I'll be calling the cops on him soon!"

He (the man) just has time to glance at the Torquemada, and the dark lad is suddenly gone, as if he never existed, vanished!

The scrap of paper marked with folds remains in the man's hand. He reads it again: "I am a Romanian Refugee . . ."

Who will write a new message for him? How can we forgive life?

   *

Around noon, he decides to give it a try. He goes into a local eatery. Considering his present situation, he hasn't got much to lose.

He tastes new and unfamiliar dishes. It's quite an experience to have one's senses subjected to the onslaught of all those spices brought together in a single dish. At first, he finds it unpleasant but ends up conceding that it is not all that bad and, in truth, is almost won over.

E *finita la comedia*. The Pauline expedition has come to an end. He decides to go back.

   *

He doesn't try to avoid passing Beaubourg on his way. He even goes off on a few tangents here and there, like a proper foreigner.

Yet the brief glimpse he got of that incredible pandemonium has been more than enough. He's turning the place back over to its original tenants. Soaked in soft twilight, the colorful city soon fades. The usual sad, lonely complexion quickly returns to everything. Back on uncertain footing, the world has once again become a heavy load to bear. That is the Paris he (the man) is now walking through.

But he'll never make it, not without fully realizing that he's already reached the point of no return on all counts, the point where everything is simply the agony of wanting to die yet not knowing how to.

III

Days go by, and nights as well. And everything seems to be going along just fine. That's what he (the man) thinks. Also, you can get used to just about anything.

Today he'd hardly strayed from the banks of the Seine. He'd started out by going to soak up some sun at the new esplanade that had recently been fixed up outside of Notre Dame. Sitting on one of the stone benches, he spent the whole morning enjoying an endlessly repeated spectacle — crowds of people gushing in, draining out, being channeled off to one side by different currents that also seemed intended to block their passage, disperse them. Tourists, all of them, or almost all, in more of a hurry to click the shutters of their cameras than to truly look at anything. The man doesn't believe he noticed a single one of them lifting their eyes to really observe Notre Dame.

In truth, he had contemplated the precision of the rotating crowds just as he did everything else — rather absent-mindedly. He had been seized by a strange kind of blankness over which he had no control. He hadn't felt overwhelmed by it or, to the contrary, as if he dominated it: he was simply in a sort of limbo in which he could clearly perceive all desires, face any and all of life's hardships with absolute calm and an underlying feeling of happiness or whatever one wished to call it. He hadn't noticed how late it was getting.

After that, he had sauntered along by the river in that same state of mind. He went into another bistro to eat a sandwich and use the toilet. Coming out, he headed back toward Notre Dame. This time he went to sit in the rundown, withered garden around the base of the cathedral. Flocks of young children were larking about under the watchful eye of their mothers amid as many flocks of sparrows and pigeons. From his post on a bench (made of wood here), he devoted his entire attention to observing them, just as the women were doing.

*

Night is already spreading out over Paris, and over the Seine too, the way it usually does — in scattered little pockets of lights and darks that, having stolen in through secret doors, give the signal for the play of invisible mirrors, in which darkness reflects light and light reflects darkness as far out as one dare look, to commence.

Once again, the land that had granted him asylum calls out to him, and so he (the man) turns toward that fixed and henceforward memorable place in which he had killed, by drowning, his name and everything that went with it. He makes his way back down to the river. From a distance in this veiled darkness, the thing intrigues him. Then, it becomes more clear as he draws nearer until he is finally upon it. It is a shape stretched out on his bench. He examines it more closely. The swell of the hip is quite pronounced in relation to the waist: it's a woman. She is lying on her right side with her knees slightly tucked up. In the dim light reflecting off the Seine, he can make out the dress pulled down to the ankle to cover her legs. Over that dress, a light summer coat hangs open with one flap sagging down to the ground.

He doesn't dare breathe, even his heart is silent. Leaning over her, he observes: quite young, probably not thirty yet, her hands are clasped under her cheek, she's sleeping without a worry in the world, not even for her own safety. He won't awaken her.

He walks away.

As if molded from the very mist itself, the image of her trails along with him, or rather, it floats before him as he guides his steps toward Pont-Neuf. But before he is able make any real progress, a voice reaches his ear. The persistence of vision ceases, its image dissolves.

It is a grotesquely hoarse voice emanating from the dense concentration of shadows collected under the bridge and bouncing up off the water, which unquestionably amplifies its gruffness. The man continues walking toward it and soon enters the darkness that, once under the bridge, seems only natural. From within those shadows, the voice is speaking to a hypothetical audience, and the speechmaker is apparently quite long-winded.

So he (the man) instinctively searches for a comfortable spot up against the pier, not far away, and sits down. The voice, far from being discreet, immediately growls in his ear: "Hey you, the new guy, don't you know that the damp saps your foundations? Here!"

The faceless voice without the slightest hint of irony had actually addressed him in quite a friendly tone.

It resumes: "We've been watching you. Being on the bum is something you gotta learn, and you sure haven't learned much yet."

A hearty laugh follows.

Lifting himself up, he (the man) slips the long piece of cardboard that was passed to him under his buttocks.

The voice begins again, equally thick: "Hey, now what was it they call you again?"

He considers the question. As a matter of fact, what name could he use? He's the man without a name. Nobody calls him anything anymore. What can he answer? He says: "The Misfit."

He didn't find the question any more misplaced than the friendly tone with which the voice spoke to him.

"You must mean The Merry Misfit? Not bad, not bad at all."

The voice has now made him feel very warm inside. "Yes, that's what I meant to say, The Merry Misfit."

Down in this pit of blackness, the disembodied voice has just given him his new name, his real name.

"Yes," he repeats, feeling no desire to add anything else — it would be completely unnecessary.

He can sense the others breathing all around him, on either side, in front of him too. How many are there?

Then the voice again: "If you stick around here, you'll be known simply as Merry. What do you think of that? Is it long enough for you?"

Merry acquiesces: "I'd be the last one to complain. It is more than enough."

And in a whisper he says again: "More than enough."

The memory of the woman lying on his bench over there comes back to Merry's mind.

"Now it's become her bench. But we'll see about that in the morning."

"Why are you being so quiet, Merry? Haven't you got anything to say?"

"There's a new day in the making, a brand new day. And, 'he laughs longest, who laughs the last.'"

"Hallelujah!"

The streetlamps shining out like that on either side of the bridge from both banks look like a light in the wilderness.

Amria and the Frenchman

Coming up to him, she murmurs in his ear: "Grandfather, you should have seen it!" *(Telling him, an old blind man, that he should have seen this or that was the kind of remark that probably no one paid any attention to anymore, and he'd be the last to take offense, perhaps because he hadn't always been blind — it was something that had happened gradually, later on in his life. Even now, he's still under the impression that his sight is only failing but that he can still see — still see things, albeit rather vaguely, from a bit farther away, from farther and farther away. But what of it? What could he reply? Those kind of things just sort of crop up in conversations, so he always says yes. Yes, because he sees what you're talking about — the point you're trying to make — that is, if you take the trouble to explain it, to choose the right words, as he is hoping his granddaughter is going to do right now, and so he waits patiently, sitting there in the sunshine like that, the bright, spring sunshine. Soaking up the sunshine, not sitting on a real bench but on a rough-hewn log lying along one wall of the little house that they all live in, he and what is left of his family. Then, he doesn't lose his patience, but he stops waiting, gets nervous, his gnarled fingers twisting about the handle of his cane, which is more like a thick stick, slightly curved at one end. He asks, fluttering his eyelids — and it isn't due to the sun shining right in his face either, they just flutter on their own accord, it's a tic he'd acquired along with his blindness, and he's perfectly aware of it when it happens, but he can't help it, can't keep himself from doing it — he asks, and his eyelids bat even harder, faster):*

"What, my little angel, seen what?"

Amria has already knelt down in front of him, and letting go of his cane, without hesitating, he puts his hands around her head as if he were holding something extremely precious, like one of those Nédromah jars one has to be so careful with, and the handsome young slip of a girl, with her head being held in that way, repeats pantingly in a low whisper: "You should've seen, you should've seen it."

"Yes, I know. Calm down, child." *(Calm down, he also repeats as he gently smoothes her hair.)*

Just then, a call — very brief, very strident — rips through the upper layers of sky. It's a swallow, one of the first to appear, and it is proclaiming its joy at being back, at having all that sky to itself, and with that message delivered, it swoops off and is entirely engulfed in blue. Then, the heavy fragrance of the flowering vineyards descends upon them, wafting in on a furtive gust of wind from the Grammont Domaine. *("Good day, sweet swallow. God bless you, swelling stems," thinks the old man affectionately. But he hasn't been able to ignore feeling how his granddaughter is shaking with anxious trembling: like a leaf. He tries to calm that leaf down — he holds Amria's head firmly between his hands. The child cannot contain her quivering, cannot find her words. He speaks to her, runs his fingers through her hair, reassures her. To encourage her, he says):* "Tell me about it. Tell me, Amria. I'm listening."

"You should've seen . . . No, I mean . . . I mean, you'll never believe what I saw! Oh my God, what I saw!"

"What is it then, my little sparrow? Tell me." *(And as his dead eyes stare out at the morning sun beating down on the dazed land, the old man pats the young girl's head that now lies in his lap.)* "What did you see, Amria?"

Her voice is filled with terror: "The Frenchman . . . He was there. I saw him . . ."

"The Frenchman! Now, now, child, calm down."

"He was exactly the same. I've seen him before. Twice now. But just a glimpse. He's back. I saw him. Saw him, I saw him . . ."

"You saw him, but where?" *(He knows that if he doesn't believe her and it shows, either in the tone of his voice or in some other way, her feelings will be terribly hurt. And that is out of the question, he can not hurt her.)* "Where did you see him?"

"Down there. At the Gramo Domaine. He's still there." She'd said Gramo, just like everyone in the village did, and not Grammont.

The old man considers that he should at least have the right to be surprised: "At the Gramo Domaine?" *(Reflecting on the matter, he* thinks: "Gramo doesn't exist anymore. The domaine is there, we still call it the Gramo Domaine, but they've all gone. The Gramos and all the others too. Quite some time ago now! Back in those days it hadn't dawned on Amria to come into the world yet, and she's twelve now. At least, I'm pretty sure she is. Even her father was but a young stripling then, and I . . . I still had my eyes. They'd just all up and left — men, women, children, everyone but the beasts and that big dog of theirs. There's not a Frenchman left in the whole length and breadth of this land. But we still call it the Gramo Domaine — even Amria, who never knew what it was like. It will always be the farm, the Gramo Domaine, even to her, because even though they're gone, a part of them lives on there. In a way they're still the masters. It's not something you can see but something you feel, and that something watches over their land, reinforces their claim to the estate. It's like a tie that's never been broken. A pact. Amria has laid her head down on my knees — she's still a child in need of protection. From what? What kind of protection? Between the two of us, which one actually protects the other? She tickles me sometimes, but today I'll have a laugh on my own. I'll keep patting her on the head like the good little filly she is and ask her): "What exactly did he look like, this Frenchman that you saw?"

She responds with a whine, "What did he look like?"

"How do you know it's a Frenchman and not someone from around here?"

"It is a Frenchman!"

"But you've never seen a Frenchman in your whole life. How can you know what one looks like?"

She lifts her head and from where she is kneeling observes the kind face lost in the riotous, fleecy beard, which was not yet entirely white but rather gray, even black in places. The eyes are the only bright, strangely alive thing in that face. It strikes her that blind people's faces are lit with an inner light, an inner light that nourishes them. She answers, but she is much calmer now: "I may have never seen a Frenchman, but I know perfectly well what they look like. And that was a Frenchman I saw all right! I would swear to it, Grandfather."

After having said her piece, she turns her head to one side, lays it back down in the old blind man's lap, and resumes: "I couldn't tell if he was an adult. But then I couldn't really say he was a child either. He was neither one. He was quite tall, yet he had such a baby-like face, not to mention that shock of curly, yellow hair on his head, like a mop of coils falling down over his eyes." *(The grandfather, recovering the sight of his past, gradually recognizes the person she is describing, whether a man or a child. He recognizes him precisely from those curls hanging down in his eyes. The name will come back to him soon. Then finally, it comes):*

"Master Jacques," he says out loud.

"What did you say, Grandfather?"

(The old man, picking up his train of thought again, ruminates: "It's the Gramo boy." Then he says): "No, nothing."

Amria goes on with her story, "He kept running along behind the fence. From one end to the other, he'd run back and forth and then start all over again. He was behind that hedge of thuja in the Gramo Domaine. He was running along by the hedge as if he were playing hide and seek and had found someone to play with. But you could tell that he was also looking for a way out, a passageway. It was a game, and yet it wasn't really fun. It was hard to tell whether he was playing or what he really wanted, but one thing was clear: he was a prisoner of the Gramo Domaine and was trying desperately to get out, escape. Every now and again he would scurry off toward the house, then return. He'd come back running at top speed and fling himself against the barrier of thuja. No, Grandfather, now I realize that he wasn't trying to hide, and come to think of it, he wasn't really playing either when he would come back and throw himself against the hedge. He was looking for a doorway, Grandfather! And the only thing he found was that long hedge of thuja stretching out as far as he could see. He didn't know where the entrance was or even that the main gateway existed. Only the fence separated us. Grandfather, you should've seen how his eyes shone — like the blue flame of the gas burner. And they kept flashing a joyous smile at seeing me there — I swear, joyous — and at the same time not really joyous at all. It was like, I don't know, it was totally different — it was like a wild type of joy, especially after he noticed I was standing there. When he looked at me, I could feel the blue flame of the gas burner licking at my skin, licking at my soul. Yet I could think of only one thing — getting away from there — but my feet refused to move. They were stuck, frozen to the spot. I was so scared, and those looks he kept darting in my direction, re-appearing each time in a different place than where I had seen him last and where I was expecting to see him again, threw me into such a panic that I felt as if I were chained to the ground."

(The old man almost asks her, "But why did you ever go near that place? Was it a jennya that led you there? Perhaps it is you who are the jennya?" But then he changes his mind — Amria is no jennya. He simply murmurs, "God, help us! It's Master Jacques ... Master Jacques himself — The baby boy I used to carry around in my arms all the time, who is now a grown lad, a lost soul. That's who my little Amria saw. Master Jacques, the Gramo boy.")

The swallow suddenly sweeps back into the sky. It cuts across the bright storm of space in a prolonged whir, marking it with a long scratch as if with a glass cutter.

"Oh Grandfather, you should've seen it. You would have wept to see your granddaughter so terror-stricken. It seemed as if he wanted to play with me — yes, that's it, play — as if he knew who I was, yet at the same time he had that frightening, lost look of some-one who doesn't recognize a soul. I've never seen anything like it. It was as if he knew me or recognized me, but that was impossible, and that's what scared me the most."

(The old man: We saw them leave. Monsieur Gramo and Monsieur Gramo's father, the boys, the women. All of them. The steward and his family. Every last one of them–the old folks as well as the young ones. After that, the domaine was de-serted. Orphaned. We were the only ones left to watch over it. But at the last minute Master François — who had always spoken to us as if he and no one else were the true Master even though he was only the steward — brought us all together and started giving us instructions, still treating us as if we were totally incompetent and explaining things we'd known all of our lives: "Be careful about this, be careful about that. Kader, don't forget to irrigate the oranges. Hey, Dahmane," — he was talking to me — "the grapes will ripen early this year, so look after them for me and

get the picking done in time. Do you understand what that means — in time? The vats need to be washed out too. Before the picking starts. You. Miloud. You're in charge of harvesting the corn, and don't wait for it to dry up on the stalk when the hot season comes. And all of you, watch the orchards, the cherries, apricots, peaches. Don't leave them hanging on the trees. Take turns keeping an eye on the houses and watering the flowers." He went on like that, Master François did, for a good long time, and regardless of what he said we would answer yes. Yes, we answered, as we had always answered. What will you say to the person who comes to wash your dead body when you happen to find yourself in his keeping? Yes! You'd have thought they were only leaving for a short time, Master François and the others, and that they would soon be coming back. They'd done that before, but never all of them at once; this time it seemed completely different, we had good reason to be worried. And yet we still weren't really convinced, deep down inside, that once they'd spent the allotted amount of time wherever they were going to spend it, they would not come back. The tone of Master François's voice would have been different if that were the case. And then they all went away leaving everything behind: the main residence, the adjacent quarters and outbuildings, the machines, the entire domaine, from one end to the other, the farm animals, and that big dog too, a huge black dog that started howling in all directions as soon as they had gone. None of us dared to go near the dog after that, though we'd all been on friendly terms with him before. He would snarl and bare his fangs at us, the workers on his own farm. He still allowed us to come into the domaine but growling all the while and watching our every move out of the corner of his eye. Can you call that a dog? More like the hound from hell! We all had the feeling that something was not right with the animal: it was going mad. Each day it got gradually worse, reverting a little further into savageness. We didn't wait for it to tear one of us apart before closing the iron gates and deciding not to go back there any more. Go back there? After that, anyone foolhardy enough to go near the place would have had that dog at their throat and been ripped limb from limb. An evil curse seemed to lay over the Gramo Domaine, and from then on the huge mad dog was its uncontested lord and master. As a matter of fact, when the men from the Management Committee came to take possession of the estate and everything else, the dog had given them such a hearty welcome that they hadn't even dared go through the main entrance. They stood outside the gate looking over the property without trying to go any further, not even as far as the front garden that was overgrown with weeds. Those very same gentlemen, or others that looked just like them, came back armed with rifles. They shot the dog and then left again having finished their day's work. It wasn't until two days later that we saw whole gangs of people arrive, saw them open the main gate and then all the doors and windows of the houses. We watched the whole operation from a distance; no one had deemed it necessary to ask our opinion about anything. It didn't matter. The buildings and the domaine had changed so much we no longer recognized them, and they didn't seem to recognize anyone either. We don't really know what happened after that. To my mind, something surely must have happened for them to have just abandoned everything in mid-stream like that. And now, fifteen years later, it's not the master who has come back but his son, Master Jacques. What's become of Monsieur Gramo? Is it possible that he's dead and gone? He wasn't anywhere near that old though. Maybe it was losing the domaine that killed him? Land runs in the veins. It's part of one's very lifeblood, and when we are torn from it that part counts for the whole. And just supposing it isn't fatal, supposing you do survive, you become nothing more than the shadow of a soul nursing its wounds. The very name you would have given that land of yours becomes a hollow shell haunted with ghostly voices. They say that even the Sahara desert has its guardians. Amria is absolutely right to think she had run into a phantom. But why the phantom of Master Jacques, the son, and not the father? He must have come at Monsieur Gramo's bidding, to carry on his work, as if the son could take charge of the land in the absence of the true master.

"Grandfather, Grandfather! Are you listening to what I'm saying or not?"

Taking hold of her grandfather's knees, Amria shakes them roughly from side to side.

"Ho! Easy there, my little dove, easy! I've been listening to everything you say," he says in a changed, distant voice.

She is just about to ask him what the meaning of that new voice could be when a *fellah* comes trotting up the dirt path digging his heels into the sides of a heavily loaded donkey. Without taking his eyes from them, he rides by, continues along his way.

Finally, he asks, "Got a problem, Uncle Dahmane?"

"Not at all, El Ghouti, not at all. Go in peace."

"All right, if you're sure . . ."

"Of course. Everything is fine."

The man urges his mount on with great bellowing cries of "Yeeha! Yeeha!"

The old man: *"May we all watch over one another, and may the angels watch over us all."*

Taking a deep breath, he says to his granddaughter, "On your feet, Amria. Let's go see what this is all about."

Just then, another Amria appears in the doorway of the small house, an Amria who has blossomed, a carbon copy of the first, a perfect reproduction. The full oval of the face, the proud, dimpled chin, the coral-colored lips curling at the corners, above all, the look in her eye, those dark, lustrous eyes veiling a rather disturbing and reserved smile, very remote, deep down under the wide arc of the brows, and this last detail, probably more than anything else, explains why the mother can be taken for her daughter's twin, barring a slight difference in age, and also they had the same bronze complexion — their faces, arms, and legs were the color of bread toasted to a golden brown.

Like Amria, she too calls the old blind man Grandfather.

"But Grandfather, where are you off to like this? We're going to eat soon. Now Amria, it's time to eat, child."

Right down to the voice with those unintentionally bantering intonations: they are Amria's. The natural order of comparison hasn't been respected, but it just so happens that the little girl appeared first and then the mother.

The old man answers, "Oh really, Saadya? We're going to check on something not far from here. We'll be back before you can get lunch on the table. Give us a few minutes to go see about this. It's just past the fountain. We won't be long. Are you coming, Amria?"

Standing on the doorstep of the house, Saadya watches them walk away and shakes her head. Seeing Amria cowering at her grandfather's feet had struck her as quite strange. What were those two up to now? She hasn't a single reason to be worried but just about every reason to be dying of curiosity. In the end, respect for the privacy of others prevails. She pockets her questions and covers them over with her handkerchief. Everything always comes out sooner or later. She'll just have to be patient. After casting one last glance at her father-in-law and her daughter walking away hand in hand, she goes back into the house.

Amria and her grandfather have already left the makeshift, box-like houses washed with a pathetic coat of blue or white behind them. They passed the fountain some time ago too. The Grammont Domaine is a little bit farther than her grandfather had let on. Amria was fully aware of that, but she hadn't wanted to quibble with him over it. His blindness has probably caused distances to take on different dimensions.

The sky is so very bright at this time of day that everything else seems muted: the wine-red soil in the fields, the copper green of the vegetation. A faint, pulsating tremor is running through that sky, through the crisp, clear light and the air too.

Amria and her grandfather reach the fountain with the elongated basin that is used for a trough and go past it. The dust in the track grows thicker, resembling the lees of wine more every minute, covering over their feet as they tramp along. The old man's stick sinks silently into it.

In passing, Amria hardly even glances at the two buckets she had dropped there a little while ago in her frightened haste.

Then they arrive at the road that runs across the dirt track. Crazily straight, it is a road that comes streaming up from one distant end of the horizon only to go rolling out toward the other. Amria stops. She carefully scrutinizes the deserted perspective of the road and dutifully retains the old man.

Finally, she leads him on, and they both stride quickly across. Having reached the other side, they pick up what is, or what should be, the continuation of the dirt track only now it has become an asphalt path leading to the Grammont Domaine. The old man readjusts his gait to the resounding sound of his stick tapping on the hard surface.

All at once, the little girl draws closer to his side. The Grammont Domaine. The barrier that runs around the property is visible. The old man senses the fear gripping Amria again. He gives the soft, slippery hand he is holding a few reassuring little squeezes.

Cautiously, they approach the dark hedge of thuja running along at eye level, beyond which the vineyard, with its infinite rows of woody stems, begins, the immense green eye of this vast land bathed in its own light.

Now it is Amria's turn to tug at her grandfather's hand. He answers back with those little squeezes, his way of saying: "Yes, I know, we've reached the Grammont Domaine." Also his way of reassuring her.

In a voice which is completely unfamiliar to Amria, her grandfather abruptly launches into a flood of gentle murmurings. It is the exact same tone of voice one would use to speak to a young child, to avoid scaring him.

"Master Jacques . . . Master Jacques . . . Are you there? It's only me, Dahmane. Do you remember? Of course you do! Well listen, if you're behind the hedge, come on out in the open, son. I've got something to say to you. This is my granddaughter that's come along with me; her name is Amria. Since you didn't mind coming out for her, come on out for me now, Master Jacques . . . Master Jacques . . ."

Old Dahmane waits a few minutes, then starts in again; his voice is kind and full of affection: "Master Jacques, its Dahmane here. We're old friends now, isn't that right? There's no one here but the two of us: Amria — who's grown into a fine young girl already — and I. Besides, I could just as well call you my son too."

He waits again. The minutes pass. Nothing happens, no answer comes from the other side of the fence. Standing there with her mouth hanging open, Amria is also waiting. She inhales, then holding in the air, stops breathing and waits some more before breathing again. Her eyes grow larger, darker, open wider.

The grandfather resumes his conversation with the nonexistent man behind the hedge. "You don't want to come out, Master Jacques? Why not? There's nothing to be afraid of. Especially if it's because you're afraid for me to see you. I lost my eyesight long ago! Maybe you didn't know that. But if you let me hear your voice, I'll be able to see you with my heart. It would be exactly as if I were really seeing you. Seeing you with your head full of tousled curls and your little round face. Come on now son, let's hear the sound of your voice, say a few words to Old Dahmane. And if you really don't want to say anything, Master Jacques, at least come a little closer.

The inflections that childhood's paradise takes on to refresh the world's memory. Hanging on that voice, Amria waits, waits to be confronted with the unbearable sight which she knows she must now face again.

"Come a little closer. Listen to what I want to ask you: why did you come back? What happened? Your whole family is gone — there's not a single person left, and you know it. You do know that, don't you? What made you come back? Is it because, even after all these years, you haven't forgotten anything? That's not good for you, son. You need to go back to where you came from. There is no one left for you here. No one but your old friend Dahmane, but I don't have much longer to live. And then who would you have? Who would recognize you or treat you as if you belonged here? Even though you do belong here. I know, you'll tell me that your trees are here, that your vineyard, your house, your land, and your sky are all still here. But there are none of your people. Did you see how frightened my little Amria was just from getting a glimpse of you? You'd scare everyone else too — you'd be nothing more than a ghost to them. It's different for me, but I'll be going soon too. I've put in my time now. You and I are lost souls, Master Jacques, and the exile of the soul is the worst kind of all. Go now, son, forget everything here. Go now and find happiness among your own kind.

I'll miss you, and though my blind eyes prevent me from seeing you, they will forever cherish the image of the beautiful child you were. Go now, Master Jacques, my son, I beg of you."

The old man simply stands there, silently facing that which he can no longer see: the hedge of thuja, the vineyard beyond with its tufted rows fading off into the distance in which, at regular intervals, olive trees also lift their silvered manes to be tousled by the quick gusts of wind in the light of that blinding sun.

He and his granddaughter are still standing there when, all of a sudden, with back arched, hair standing on end, hissing, and showing its fangs, a cat springs from the hedge and comes shooting toward them with all its claws out. Instinctively, the grandfather brandishes his stick. Amria gives a startled cry, but before she can even think of jumping out of the way, not a trace of the cat or even its shadow. Vanished, but leaving behind the feeling that the air is charged with some strange kind of electricity.

Amria's face has turned very red — the whole landscape is throbbing before her eyes. She notices that her grandfather is frozen to the spot, just as she is, and seems to be assailed by all sorts of incredible thoughts.

The old man lays his hand on her shoulder. He presses down lightly, and she understands immediately. It is no longer in their power to change anything. It's time for them to go back home now.

Silently, they turn and start back.

The path they are taking might lead back toward the house, but it is also taking the old man a long way back in time. He finds himself back at the Grammont Domaine in the midst of the busy life they used to live there. He's hurrying around, going from one chore to the next, having recovered his eyesight. And that little mischief-maker with his head full of corkscrew curls comes running up and bumps right into his knees. The child wants to be picked up again.

Amria collects the buckets in passing and fills them at the fountain.

With a bucket hanging from each arm, she joins the old man who is waiting for her, lost in thought, and together they start off again. She, with short, quick steps, trying not to spill a single drop from the buckets, and he, tap-tapping his way along with his stick. The rich, golden light surrounding them is so thick it is almost palpable.

Saadya is waiting for them, and lunch has been on the table for quite some time.

Talilo Is Dead

The doorbell to the apartment rings. Who could that be? I'm not expecting anyone today. The mailman? That's impossible — he only comes in the morning, and it's two o'clock in the afternoon. I leave my work and go to answer the door. None of my friends would have rung the bell like that. Everyone knows I never lock the door — they just turn the handle and walk in. Sometimes they give a short ring beforehand, just as a sort of anticipatory greeting.

At the open door, a fairly young woman stands before me. That blonde face, which, as far as the half-light on the landing reveals, would be round if it weren't for the curved brackets of her jaw line coming together to form a tulip-shaped chin, is unfamiliar to me. From her expression, her attitude, and God knows what else, it's obvious she expects me to recognize her. Yet the face just doesn't ring a bell. I've got so much work piled up these days, I don't really feel like playing guessing games.

She remains there, planted imperturbably in front of me, wearing a sober blue suit. Is she going to explain the reason for this visit?

Finally, she introduces herself: "I'm Aëlle."

Hearing that name almost makes my heart jump into my throat.

"Aëlle?" I respond faintly.

"Yes, may I come in?"

"Yes, of course, excuse me. Come in. Come in, please."

I step back and allow her to enter. From the main hall, I show her into the living room, which is flooded with light and sunshine. Aëlle walks resolutely over to an easy chair and sits down with her back to the picture window. I could tell at first glance that she wouldn't sway from that odd sort of determination with which she is now putting that darkened face between her and the room, between her and me.

Before sitting down myself, I ask her: "Can I offer you something to drink?"

"If it's a cup of tea, yes, I would love one," she replies without hesitation.

It is then that I notice the faint accent that betrays her foreign origins.

I leave her alone for a few minutes to go and prepare the tea.

She watches me as I come back into the room and set the large cup I am holding down in front of her. Then I take a seat on a sofa in the corner, facing her.

For the moment, she contents herself with saying: "And you? Aren't you having anything?"

That accent. I know what it reminds me of now.

"No, I couldn't. I just finished my coffee."

I have barely pronounced those innocuous words when she adds: "Talilo is dead."

"Talilo? Great gods!"

She clarifies: "He committed suicide."

Like the repeated, choppy slosh of waves in a stormy sea, memories come washing up over me, and along with the images of Talilo, from the blurred recesses of a very old story, flashes of Aïd also come to the surface, flashes of Doderick and Rouka, of Saskör and . . . Aëlle. The very same Aëlle who is sitting there in front of me and saying, "Surely you'll remember telling me that after the evening spent on the island, he tried to kill himself but had failed. Well, not long ago, he succeeded. He's gone and killed himself."

As she relates the tragedy, she is totally detached. Her voice has taken on the intonations of a messenger who does not feel in the least implicated in the message he bears. It deeply disturbs me. As she begins telling the story, she stops staring at me, and instead, her eyes seem to be gazing upon something only she can see. Now that her eyes are back in their normal perspective, I can observe their natural greenness, encrusted with tiny diamonds that make them glisten even when they are at rest. Like a sparkling stream I sit contemplating, just as Aïd — Ed — had done.

A shudder runs through me, and if I succeed in remaining outwardly calm, it isn't in the least due to any extraordinary willpower on my part but rather to the fact I am overcome with a feeling of emptiness; my whole being is numb. I can see Talilo standing up straight and tall — massive, but without really being as extremely tall as one imagines people of his size to be; always wearing those same tight-fitting overalls with his belly sticking out, not outrageously so, but beginning under his double chin and bulging out all the way down to his thighs. As soon as you noticed the smile in his little twinkling eyes, you quickly forgot his awkwardness and his corpulence too. It was the benevolent, gentle, understanding smile of utter devotion, of a readiness for self-sacrifice simply to please you. No animal will ever be that devoted, although in this regard, they've always been superior to human beings and more gifted as well.

The very first time I met Talilo, I felt a bond of friendship between us, real friendship that was reciprocal. And because of it, I am all the more horrified at having prophesied his death. I must add here, though, that I did nothing more than tell a story. But it isn't all that simple to get off the hook. The more I think of him and the fatal act he was driven to commit, the less I can forgive myself. I was the one who pointed the man out, he who was in the full bloom of life. I condemned him to his fate.

As though she has read my mind, or more precisely, as if she's been thinking the very same thing, Aëlle speaks up: "You simply finish telling your story, relating the events, and then you close the book. For you, it's all over with. Everything stops there. You turn the page. You don't even think about what might happen to the people you lived through the story with, but for them the game isn't over. They still have to roll with the punches, regardless of whether you're there or not, just like Talilo had to, right up until he threw himself into the arms of death. Of course you'll say you had no idea that you were pushing him to do it. That might well be so, but in the end, it doesn't really make any difference whether you did it deliberately or not."

Aëlle is gathering evidence for her case against me. She has no idea that I am in complete agreement with her, that I admit my guilt, and that I'd be the last person on earth to try and defend myself.

I turn toward her, and she fixes those eyes on me again, yet at the same time she seems to be looking beyond, at something else — Aëlle has often given me that impression. I ask, "Could you tell me a little more about his death?"

No answer.

After nearly a full minute of cold impassiveness, she retorts, "Do you think that people who decide to kill themselves send out invitations?"

I listened to that response in utter silence. I won't ask her any more questions. She's told me what she came to tell me. She felt a strong obligation to do so. But in the silence that fell between us, the specter of Talilo's voice, and that of Aïd also, and the others, began to arise.

Aëlle is already standing, ready to leave.

    *

Alone, the thoughts running through my mind all seem, in one way or another, to lead back to Talilo's death. There are people who die in this world that we don't feel in any way responsible for. So why does the death of someone like Talilo disturb me so much? Did I not love him enough? And had I loved him more, would he have spared himself this violent death? I did love him very much, yet that, of course, depends upon how one estimates the amount of love he has to give. The need for love, on the other hand, is impossible to evaluate. His was in all likelihood enormous, far exceeding the capacity to give, and that is what killed him.

As for Aëd, Aëlle had preferred to remain silent. An odd sort of silence. How can it be explained? She'd never once mentioned Aëd's name. Could it be she simply had nothing say? Obviously, she hadn't come to talk about him.

*

Ever since Aëlle's visit, eight or ten days ago now, not a day has gone by that I haven't thought of her and the sad news that she brought, that she'd felt duty-bound to bring me in person. There has hardly been a day in which I haven't pictured her sitting there like that, with her back to the window, which made her stand out like a dark statue, and recalled the way those shadows magnified her presence, especially when her eyes shone and flashed out, saying so much more than words, or even silence, ever could.

And today I find a letter from her in the morning mail. Without really daring to hope, I'd expected at least that much from her. I'll be damned if it still doesn't make a lump rise in my throat, just to think about it!

Coincidentally, and with that infallible intuition of hers, Aëlle writes, among other things:

"You must have found it strange that I didn't mention Ed. I suppose it was difficult for you to understand, and you wondered why. I find it hard to answer that question: I hadn't come to talk about him. He's still at the house — he's doing as well as can be expected. He doesn't go out much, but when the weather is fine, he manages to get himself down into the garden. Sometimes he stays quite a long time.

"I told him about Talilo's death, of course.

"'Was it someone I knew?' he asked worriedly.

"What could I have said?

"I answered, 'No.'

"However, I'm not at all certain that my denial made him feel any better. Several times during the day, he brought the subject back up and begged me to tell him more about this Talilo fellow.

"He keeps himself busy. He's always taking notes. He fills pages and pages with them, and at least once a month, he gathers them into a sort of report that he slips into an envelope and asks me to post for him.

"The addresses on the envelopes are invariably the same: the offices of diverse ministries, back in a city called Orsol.

"Then, a week or so goes by, and I watch his normally calm appearance change into anxious expectation. A feverish expression comes over his face, and he can't concentrate on what he's doing anymore. He seems to be going around in circles until, for the sake of restoring his peace of mind, feigning indifference when the mail comes, he asks if there was anything in his box.

"'Yes, but just a bunch of circulars,' I'm obliged to answer.

"Then, his face will fall ever so slightly, or he'll stare at me with a questioning look that is heart-wrenching, and his expression changes. He assumes that distant, impenetrable look once again. It's as if he has returned to the place he had briefly escaped from, a world to which he alone has the key.

"A little bit later, he, who so rarely speaks anyway, goes silently back to his notes.

"I now confess that my curiosity finally got the better of me; I gave in and looked through his papers. Since then, every document he mails is routed through my desk, where they all remain, stowed safely away. They are so much more precious to me than they will ever be to him. It is a treasure I'll always keep within arm's reach, that I would never part with, no matter what.

"You may judge for yourself from the examples I am enclosing; I can only send photocopies, please don't ask for anything more. Besides, I'm only doing it for Ed and to please you.

"My love for Ed grows deeper every day. I can't imagine what would become of me without him . . ."

Aëlle had in fact included some pages in her letter, but I can only remember certain passages, which I will do my best to reproduce here:

It's one of those lakes that I'm speaking of now. Above the lake, beyond the semi-circle of hills still cloaked in a luxuriant green, though summer is nearing its end — take heed, winter will soon be upon us! — hovers the vast, vibrant sky. Contemplate that sky, then observe the placid water: you too will become vibrant.

And the lake gazes back at you in still silence. Like an omniscient eye opening on the beyond, and, mesmerized by that gaze, even your remotest aspirations to happiness are renewed — you find yourself believing in the power of that water, which might just as easily send you hurtling back toward the past as forward, toward an already existent future. You are the hope that it's trying to retrieve.

If you recognize that water, it will recognize you in turn.

My life seems to be filled with its light, seems to have nearly been atoned for.

    *

Even if someone's days are numbered, it doesn't detract from the revelation. Admitting it to oneself, discussing it in a soulful dialog with the water, immersing oneself in its coolness. The world, in its opacity has chosen to reveal itself through the transparency of this water. And we remain its shadow, the shadow it casts, the shadow that clouds it. The face of the lake is witness, but we know not to what, and our gaze, nostalgically seeks an answer. If, in universal terms, everything is of equal importance, in our eyes no two things have the same value. Where should one stand, what side should one choose to be on? The water answers this question and surges back with still more answers. The part that is us, the part that is it, the ebb and flow, divergent branches, the desire to reflect our images back at us and to incarnate them. Being, without being ourselves.

The caress: a difficult thing to do and undo. The caress: an act that both ties and releases. Everything that has been held deep within floats up to the surface, is liberated.

Self interrogation, wondering: how did I ever end up here? The circumstances under which we were taken aboard in the marina. Simply pure chance that things happened to turn out this way. No, it was not just a matter of chance that I was invited but that instead of taking me on his boat, my host left me on the dock and someone else did what he hadn't been able to. Neither was it an accident if, at the same time, a strange young woman had also been left on the dock. No, it wasn't blind luck that the providential boatman had taken both of us aboard his craft and we were unloaded on his island. It is the water that takes you by the hand and helps you find your way.

But the rest of the story has been forgotten. Forgotten somewhere along the way.

The half-light of a forest, its impenetrable, labyrinthine depths. The mysterious multitude of its silent ranks and from time to time, the sudden wildness springing from between the tree trunks. The rustling latticework of their dome arching giddily across the sky. An abandoned temple of some forgotten cult ready to be reborn at the slightest invocation. One can sense the quickness of life under there, a continual, imperceptible buzzing. One must have a reliable guide to venture in there. It reminds me of a similar place, or rather it is a memory deep within me that recalls a place like this. A curtain of green, splinters of light, thousands of hushed voices, silence that suddenly swells, and that one voice. Calling out. I listen and I remember. Although it's a very vivid memory, it is somehow impersonal.

Paquita, or The Ravished Gaze

"Señora madre, señora madre,"

"Yes, mía, . . . What is it? . . ."

"Are you listening to me, señora madre?"

"Yes, Paquita. What do you want now? Really! Why don't you call me *mama, mamita*? Like you used to.

"Like I used to?"

"Yes, like you used to! Like you used to!"

"I . . . I don't know."

"Well, go ahead. What did you want to tell me?"

"What did I want to tell you? I . . ."

"Well?"

"I can't remember."

"All right then, I suppose it wasn't all that important."

The mother laughs with the generous laughter of half-blooded Indians, and her eyes make a slit that stretches across the width of her face from one temple to the other.

She turns back to the fire she'd been tending and becomes completely absorbed in it again.

Paquita remains just as she is: standing in her corner, in the darkest part of the house.

A dank ship's hold — this room is a ship's hold, and the only light comes from the door. But it's their house, the same as all the others.

Paquita is waiting, trying to remember what she'd wanted to tell her mother, waiting for it to come back to her — or else she's waiting for something to happen.

Finally, she gives up and, in a thin voice made thinner yet by introspection or perhaps simply by dreaminess, she begins to sing very softly, apparently unconcerned at being in the semi-darkness:

113

Look at every little thing
And tell me from out there
What it is you see,
My deep black eyes.
Look at every little thing . . .

"Señora madre, señora madre, now I know, I remember!"

"What's gotten into you, why are you shouting like that? And what is it that you remember?"

"The little girls up there in the North, las gringas, they all have blue eyes. Don't they all have blue eyes?"

"I think so. And what of it? What difference does it make if they all have blue eyes?"

"And that little girl, the one whose parents bought my eyes, did she have blue eyes too?"

The mother continues blowing on the fire. She doesn't turn her head toward Paquita this time.

The little girl can feel this. She insists, "My eyes . . . to put them in the place of hers?"

The woman cannot keep herself from casting a furtive glance in the girl's direction. She's not at all certain that her daughter isn't observing her from the shadows that conceal her, the shadows from which she can tell the girl is awaiting an answer.

She says, coughing suddenly, probably from having breathed in a mouthful of smoke or maybe more, "I don't know anything about it, Paquita! Rah! Rah! Nothing about anything, rah! And what good does it do to talk about it now?"

She sneezes and coughs at the same time. Paquita pursues her idea, "It's because I was wondering how she's getting along with black eyes, she who had blue eyes before. I wonder how, with her hair as light as the sun, the kind of hair that always goes with blue eyes, how she's getting along? Do you know, señora madre?"

"Ay, ay, Paquita! I don't feel well! Blessed Virgin, help me. Nuestra Señora de Guadalupe, I beg of you! Ay, Paquita, it hurts!"

When the mother falls to a sitting position on the floor after having been squatting down for quite some time, she doesn't fall very far and yet she begins to shriek, rolling her head from one side to the other. Her two braids, which had been hanging down her back, are now whipping at her breast. Along with the shrieking comes another fit of coughing. Asunción is gasping as though she were suffocating and this were the end, as though she were about to stop breathing for good.

"Señora madre, señora madre, what's wrong? Can you hear me? Señora madre . . ."

Paquita had cried out, and she stands there listening in her corner.

Her ears are then filled with every imprecation that her mother is able to utter and, immediately afterwards, as many lamentations. Paquita imagines how she must be sitting on the bare earthen floor with her legs sprawled out. She imagines her crying, with her mouth distorted but with no tears, for she has no more tears to give. Finally, she imagines her banging her head against the floor, and now she can hear a dull thudding sound.

Still without moving from her corner, Paquita implores her, "No, señora madre! No!"

Asunción can't hear her. Her laments have changed into a long, monotonous groan, and nothing, it seems, will be able to stop it, appease it.

*

Hopping from one foot to the other, the little girl is dancing and singing:

> My night-black eyes
> That yonder take the place
> Of eyes so azure blue:
> Look closely, look closely
> At every little thing
> And tell me from out there

What it is you see,
Tell me from out there
What it is you see

My eyes that laugh,
My eyes that cry
Yonder so very black:
Here, so I may laugh,
Here, so I may cry,
I've nothing but my mouth

But cry and laugh
Yonder so very black.
Cry and laugh . . .

"Señor padre! Señor padre! Are you listening to me or not?"

"I'm listening to you, my little dove. Go ahead."

"The little gringa in her country up there in the North, she had blue eyes, didn't she, señor padre, and now she has mine and they're black?"

"Yes, my little dove."

"Are you sure?"

"Yes, my little dove."

"They didn't turn blue?"

"No, my dove, I don't think so."

Sitting in front of his house, looking out into the center of the village, Miguel is braiding a rope.

He stops. He's no longer working the hemp fibers with his fingers or braiding them either. The strand he has already twined, stretched between his fingers and toes, waits, and he's sitting there listening. Paquita is talking behind him, and he's sitting perfectly still, listening. The cool breath of morning is still in the air, the sun is still hidden behind the mountain. The mountain, of course, has not yet lifted its shadow.

Miguel repeats in his slow voice, "No, my dove. I don't think so."

"And what if they turn blue too someday? Someday. Maybe . . ."

"Don't think about that, my dove. Don't think about it anymore."

"I'd like to know."

"Don't think about it anymore, Paquita."

"Maybe they'll let me know, someday, from far away, up there in the North."

"Be quiet, my dove. Be quiet."

"But why, señor padre? You must know whether they'll tell me or not."

"Paquita!" Miguel protests.

But immediately, as if in prayer, he murmurs, "Blessed Virgin, have pity on us. Blessed Virgin, have pity on us."

The man, whose face has the shape of an antique Andean vase and is baked just as darkly, with a small pink blush at the tip of each cheekbone, turns and, with a long, fixed gaze, stares in silence at his little girl. Six years old. At least he thinks so, he can't be sure. Six years old; he thinks about what he has done to her — what they have done to her, all of them — and that it will be with her as long as she lives. She already knows too much for her age. Much too much, that's what he thinks.

After having stared for a long time into the hollows of her eyes, he says, "The Blessed Virgin will give them back to you in heaven."

"And they'll be blue, señor padre?"

The man doesn't seem to be able to find the words with which to answer her. He hesitates, then says, "I'm sure of it, my dove."

*

They're all there playing jacks in the dust — Juanita, Inès, Paloma, and Emilia. They're chattering. They're giggling.

Suddenly, accusing one another of cheating, they lose their tempers and start to fight. But just as abruptly, are friends again and resume their jabbering — cicadas chirping furiously in the height of the afternoon heat.

Paquita is standing off to herself, next to the house. She recognizes each of the girls by their voices. Even when they all start bickering at the same time in that falsetto tone of voice they deem necessary to affect, she can easily tell which of the girls says this or says that.

Right now, just like a little magpie chattering at you, Inès is calling to her, "Don't you want to come and play with us too, Paquita? Come on, instead of standing over there all by yourself!"

"I can't."

"Why? You can play jacks just as well as we can."

That's not Inès anymore — it's Juanita that just spoke.

Paquita answers again, "I can't."

"Are you mad at us or something?" Juanita asks. She becomes insistent, "Paquita, *un poquito.* Come and play *un poquito.*"

The girls' interest has centered on this conversation. They left the jacks just as they had fallen, scattered on the hard-tamped earth.

Paquita can't just let them say whatever they like to her. "How silly! I'm not mad at you! It's because I don't want to soil my pretty dress. Why should I be mad at you?"

A strange silence sets in — the light of day, the girls are holding their breath in the light of day. And Paquita, who doesn't understand what is going on, Paquita too, is holding her breath. From not breathing, she feels as though she's gradually fading out, becoming transparent.

And then it explodes: four painfully loud shrieks of laughter followed by what sounds like the cries of toucans, laughter that is not really laughter, that is like the blasts of trumpets. And then it comes back, starts up again.

"Blessed Virgin! Lord Jesus! Soil you pretty dress? Ha!"

You'd think they were crazy. That's what Paquita tells herself, and one of them, Emilia, who is crazy for sure, shouts to her, "What pretty dress? Where is this pretty dress of yours?"

"Where do you think it is, you bunch of pests! On me! I'm wearing it! Papa bought it for me in town when he went there three days ago. Papa bought it himself. He can buy anything he wants to."

"But where is this city-bought dress of yours? We'd like to admire it."

And then it's Juanita that says, "A rag like that! In that case, we're wearing even prettier dresses, ones that come from Paris!"

Even Rafaele, the village idiot, doesn't get that many laughs when they bring him out into the village square all dressed up for Mardi Gras.

Paquita isn't paying any more attention to them. She smoothes out her dress with both hands, but there's a lump in her throat.

"You can come and play, Paquita. You don't have to worry about that pretty dress of yours at all."

Turning her back on the girls, Paquita goes back into the house. Deep down in her heart, she thinks: I'll believe whatever Padre and Madre want me to believe.

Also, deep down in her heart she now sings:

My eyes, my eyes
Look at every little thing
And tell me from out there
What it is you see

Laugh, my jet-black eyes, laugh
But please not about my dress
My dress neither pretty or new
For pity's sake, I pray thee

It is a song that had been born of her grief, which is in turn forever being born and reborn from the song. But even so, there's no harm in trying again, starting all over from the beginning.

Paquita is sing-talking to the two sticks tied together in the form of a cross that she's dressing up in rags. It will be her new doll.

My eyes, laughing from out there,
The Virgin will give them back,
In heaven will give them back.

While her fingers continue to busy themselves, she interrupts her song and, in an everyday voice, a conversational voice, she asks, "Señora madre, are you there? Señora madre . . ."

Lately, she has discovered that she can sense intuitively when someone is near. Paquita knows that her mother is there. She had only asked to make conversation, without really wanting to say anything in particular.

Without a word, Asunción gets up, walks over, and, going up the three steps to the front door, steps out into sunlight, into the fresh mountain air. She doesn't go any farther than that. She can't take her eyes from the scorched earth in which only rocks can live. Not a thought enters her mind as she stands there looking out over that wasteland.

Paquita, alone now, picks up the thread of her song-talk, with her face lifted toward the door:

In heaven will give them back
And so very blue they'll be.

She continues assembling the ball of rags with her distracted and suddenly trembling fingers. She's only sing-talking for herself now, in secret. No, she knows she's doing it for someone else as well, someone whose name she won't tell:

Look at every little thing
And tell me from out there
What it is you see,
My deep black eyes.

"Señor padre, señor padre, you know something?"

"What, my dove?"

"I'll go myself, one day, go way up North to get my eyes back. I'll go from city to city, from house to house, asking people. I'll find them again with the help of the Virgin. And do you know what else?"

"No, what?"

"Even if they've turned blue, I'll recognize them."

"That's for sure, my dove. That's for sure. And I'll go with you. We'll look for them together."

"Oh, Papa!"

"It feels good to hear you say *Papa*."

"Oh, Papa, I don't even know what I look like any more."

*

The pounding of her own heartbeat awakens Paquita with a start, but it's only a dream. She just had a dream, and it's still with her, or rather she's still with it. She saw herself going to school, and then walking into the classroom, and then the other girls turned around. At first they all looked at her in utter surprise, and then their eyes slowly filled with wonder. They all came and made a circle around her, and the Mistress came to join them too. Then the Mistress said what the others, in their stunned speechlessness, hadn't been able to say.

"Bless the Lord! What lovely blue eyes you have now, Paquita! And that beautiful dress!"

*

"We live off of your eyes, Paquita. You know that."

"Yes, Papa."

Her voice had cracked when she had pronounced that *yes, Papa*, and it's hardly more than a murmur when she asks, "Do we live better now, Papa?"

"Yes, Paquita, yes."

With a flip of the tongue, Miguel changes his lump of cola from one cheek to the other. He didn't spit after that; his Adam's apple lifted in a swallowing movement, nothing more.

"But we're feeling worse and worse inside. Something is eating away at our insides. Something has already eaten away everything that was in your mother's head, and everything she does is done with that empty head of hers and is always all wrong. It's as if

121

everything we put into our mouths starts devouring us at the same time."

Paquita has never heard her father speak at such length. She doesn't try to understand why: it worries her. Her instinct tells her what she must do to ward off any evil spirits that might be prowling around them.

Brightly, she cries, "Ever since my eyes were taken away, the world has become so much vaster."

Life Today

When someone gave me a hand-out in the street the other day, I had no idea of what to do or think. It was the last thing in the world I would have expected. At first I didn't understand how I could have allowed myself to be caught off-guard like that, and my hand closed over the handsome coin that had just been slipped into my palm. Not only that, I even tried to justify it to myself: "I had been taken by surprise. It had left me so utterly speechless that the thought of refusing the coin had never even occurred to me." These excuses were entirely insincere, and I was only using them to make it easier to avoid the real question — which is to say, asking myself whether the way I looked and acted weren't more likely to inspire pity than any other sentiment. Yes, such pity that it prompts people to give you charity. That should have been my first thought, but at the time nothing of the sort entered my mind. Our lives are governed by the omnipotent force that we call destiny. It had been destiny that led me to cross the path of a benevolent man. What else was I to do but accept what had happened? There can't be anything wrong with an action that brings out the good side of human beings.

And so, I had simply accepted the fact, as I just explained, but that particular morning — which wasn't really all that long ago — was quite a memorable one. It was so wonderfully balmy — autumn had already begun, and yet, up until then the heat had been grueling. Then suddenly, the town was finally able to breathe. The two of us, Khelil and I, were sitting down comfortably, his tiny hand cradled in mine, with a first-rate view of the marketplace. We go out together every morning — it's an old habit of ours — with no other end in sight but to stroll over toward the center of town or, to be more exact, toward the market. Sitting in the doorway to a vendor's stall that I've never once seen open, we observe the lively and often quite entertaining scene unfolding before us.

If, however, amid the passersby certain people happen to appear unusual or behave in an intriguing manner, or if a quarrel begins and eventually comes to blows, then Khelil will start in on his questions. At times like these, I need to demonstrate that I am every bit as observant as he is and keep a sharp eye out in order to come up with the right answers. Nothing less will satisfy him — I know him all too well. Having said this, my grandson is not really one of those children who relentlessly besets you with the whys and hows of any little thing or, which is even more tiresome, of every little thing. He's more the silent type, pensive — maybe even a bit too much so for his mere ten years of age. The type of questions that he asks me — always so serious — are proof enough of that. I'm glad that he's already a man and not a nitwit.

I can still see him asking me on that very same morning, "Grandpa, what's . . ."

But he had barely opened his mouth when a stranger walked up to us and, without even stopping, put something in my hand. If only that hand could talk, the very hand I had unconsciously left lying open on my knee.

The person was gone before I noticed that I was holding a coin. If the fellow had feared being pursued for some sort of crime, he couldn't have vanished more hastily. My fingers curled over the flat metal disc, and I just sat there looking in the direction that I assumed he had gone.

Meanwhile, Khelil was naively repeating to my deaf ears, "Grandpa, what's . . ."

With the coin in the hollow of my hand, I kept trying to recall the face of the philanthropist that had been so incredibly generous, and I couldn't stop marveling at how deftly he had slipped away. I was willing to admit that his gesture had pleased me, but it was in a way that left me completely bewildered. The damage — I mean the good — having already been done, why should he choose to disappear rather than show his face? Out of kindness? Because I would know his name for sure. Everyone knows one another in our town, at least by sight.

"Grandpa, what did that man give you?"

If the man had done as he saw fit, there was nothing I could say about it now.

This once, Khelil wouldn't stop pestering me, "Grandpa, what did that man . . ."

In answer, I opened my hand and showed him the large coin.

Wide-eyed, the child contemplated it breathlessly, and I allowed my thoughts to drift back to the mysterious well-wisher. Then, preparing for a rash of embarrassing questions that might humiliate me, I hurriedly began to assure him, "Upon my word, son, I have no idea why he gave me this gift."

It probably wasn't at all what I should have said, but I said it, exculpating myself as if I had done something shameful that he had unwittingly accused me of. But he just sat there gazing with a look of wonder at the coin shining in the palm of my hand.

I could read the innocent, mute joy in his eyes, and I too was happy to silently share it with him. Though one question still remained, he answered it on his own, "It's because we're poor." There wasn't the slightest hint of plaintiveness in his voice — he was noting a simple fact. This was completely new to him, and he would have to live with it from then on.

I put the coin in my pocket, and the two of us concentrated on the throngs of people filing past us or on the others that were going into or coming out of the covered market. The automobiles — more numerous than we had ever seen them — were inching through the regular neighborhood crowd with great difficulty. Quite a few people in our city have grown rich since independence was declared. Good for them — as children they had probably known many a hungry day.

"But life has been good to us as well," I thought to myself. "Now we, too, are a little richer. We have this fine coin."

Whatever was I blathering on about? My head would certainly have started to swell if Khelil hadn't happened to bring me back down to earth. He was imploring, "Grandpa, can I see it one more time?"

I understood immediately what he wanted. I showed him the coin again and caught myself smiling at the way in which he contemplated it for the second time — silently and with such wide eyes.

Then the only thing that seemed to interest him was the dance of bees milling around the enormous hive of the marketplace. I admit that I was quite impressed by his show of reserve. That's my Khelil for you.

However, before long he lifted that cute little nose of his and inquired, "What will you do with the money, Grandpa?" Now that really left me speechless. You see, he had found time to think about this aspect of things, whereas I hadn't!

I was all the more impressed since I understand exactly how his mind works, and I was rather embarrassed too; all I could think to say was, "I don't really know, my boy."

Incredulous, he riveted those feverish, immensely black eyes of his on me. It was obvious he had expected a different answer, and it seemed to confuse him even more when I added, "But what do you think we should do with it? It's half yours as well."

"Half mine?"

He stood there looking at me with those eyes — those eyes that were too big, too shiny, too black — and then it seemed as if his eyes suddenly withdrew. Afterwards, when he began again, I could hear a tremor of denial in his voice.

"You'll buy some tobacco with it. The real fine-cut tobacco that looks like soft hair and that you so enjoy rolling up in those little pieces of paper. That's what you'd like, isn't it? Go ahead, admit it. You haven't smoked any for such a long time."

Now it was my turn to be startled. I didn't realize that he paid such close attention to my slightest little habits. My young Khelil is so perceptive. He never forgets anything. Of course I couldn't help thinking, "If it is your destiny to understand everything, I don't envy you in the least, my boy. It's never good to be all that intelligent in life — it only causes suffering and, furthermore, there's nothing to be gained from it. However, we can't change what was meant to be."

As I cast about for something to say, he pinned me down again with that steady gaze. "I've finally outgrown that habit now," I answered him.

He didn't intimidate me, but the look in his eyes was so touching. I started laughing in hopes that he would follow my example. But he said, "What habit?"

"The habit of smoking, obviously!"

"How can you grow out of the habit of doing something you love?"

His eyes remained defiant, watching me unblinkingly, a window opening into gaping darkness. "It is possible," I replied. "Some people do. Habits can be outgrown too."

"You had to outgrow it. Why don't you just admit it? You had to."

"Oh, had to, had to — that's not exactly the right term! Oh all right then, yes — more or less." I could have broken down and cried. I felt so wretched, so unprepared for all of this.

Laying his hand on mine, he said, "That's what I thought."

As he sat there next to me, I shot a sideways glance at him. He was the perfect image of what he should be — there wasn't a sign of hypersensitivity, pity, or resentment of any kind, no evidence of anything he would have needed to hide or keep to himself.

The uninterrupted din around us had continued to swell, growing and spreading out like rumbling thunder — the cries being called out from one stall to another, reverberating through the entrails of the ogre of the covered market; the racket with which the same ogre's eight mouths sucked up or spewed out wave after wave of men, of women; the automobiles, mired in the throngs, bleating furiously; the melodious chants of the small vendors strolling about in the street holding up a few bunches of radishes in their fists: total cacophony, a tumultuous cloud that enveloped us like a second atmosphere. I smiled confidently at Khelil without saying a word, without losing hope, but not without fearing I would end up giving something away — something that I didn't necessarily feel like divulging, that I didn't really want to say.

Then, not being able to stand it any longer, I exclaimed, "I've just had a better idea!"

It was true — I'd just had an idea, one that I could also use to cut short a conversation that I was beginning to be afraid would take a bad turn or end up causing an argument between us. We've had arguments before: sometimes Khelil has a way of seeing things, of reacting to things, that grieves me, and that's sort of what might have happened on that particular morning.

"So what is this idea of yours?" he asked.

"What if we went and bought a package of cookies, hum? The kind with the apricot filling that are wrapped in shiny gold paper with pretty pictures on it?"

At that point, he could barely manage to articulate: "Really?"

And then he turned to look out into the crowd, but was he really seeing it? He didn't say another word, and I didn't know what to do after that. I never know what to do with him.

We sat there silently watching over all of those madmen who seemed to be running around, hurrying to answer some specific request. And they all headed straight for the huge, two-storied, covered building squatting squarely in the center of the market swallowing them up from the ground floor, swallowing them up from the first floor, swallowing up as many as could pour into it, in bulk, and spitting out just as many; but only the rich mounted the monumental double staircase leading up to the first floor on each of the four sides of the building, and even though they were surrounded with an entourage of servants or porters, they hardly needed to shove their way through the crowd.

Suddenly, Khelil began to pull energetically at my sleeve. "Why is that woman shouting?"

My thoughts had been elsewhere, and I had no idea what he was talking about. I looked about. "What woman?"

"Over there. Do you see her now?"

He pointed to a middle-aged woman wearing an open haïk that had nearly slipped from her head who was shouting at the top of her lungs at a tiny man sitting in the entrance to the marketplace behind a meager display of herbs, parsley, coriander leaves, fresh mint, and cooking mint.

The answer was obvious to me, "That's the way our women are. They set their own prices with the vendor, and if he refuses to accept, they scold him. That one doesn't seem to be any exception to the rule."

But the man, despite his frailness, was putting up a louder squawk than even she was — so loud that we could hear what he was saying from where we sat.

"Go on now, woman, just get along now. You don't think I get my wares for free, do you?"

Then she, totally indignant: "A fortune for a sprig of parsley! What will become of the world with greedy vultures like you merchants? You won't be happy until you've bled us all dry! So you're building yourself a castle too, is that it? Just like all the others?"

Just then a solemn, spacious, and sparkling automobile appeared and blotted them from our view. It stopped in the very midst of the crowd and remained there — another one of those arrogant new nabobs who believes he is above all the rules, that he has the right to drive his car wherever he wishes, and even that a parking place should be reserved for him wherever he goes. He was one of those types, but he wasn't about to find that parking place here, not even if he paid for it.

And, just as you might expect, another car appeared going in the opposite direction, identical in every aspect except for its pistachio-green color — the first one was café-au-lait — another one, every bit as solemn, spacious, and sparkling as the first, inching along despite the resistance offered by the indifferent human mass, another one that also ground to a halt, just as it was passing its twin. With their windows rolled down, totally ignoring the people whose passage they were blocking and the other automobiles that had shown up in the meantime and were already beginning to hoot, the two drivers then launched into a conversation they didn't seem in the least inclined to cut short. Though there was a policeman on duty standing at a nearby corner observing the whole scene, he was so dreamy-eyed, you'd think he was on some other planet entirely.

To top everything off, the loudspeakers started blaring with an ear-splitting blast that left you totally stunned, empty of all feeling. It was the summons for the dohor prayer. Spiritual aspiration hasn't been expressed by the call of the muezzin for a long time now.

I rose to my feet not so much to obey the injunction of the screaming machine as to inform Khelil, "Young man, it's past noon. We're going home now."

He rose in turn, not taking his eyes from mine, the eyes I know so well, which, in addition to their usual intensity, were now brimming with a smile that expressed so much more than words ever could.

Yet, for fear of not being understood, Khelil translated his thoughts, saying, "You haven't forgotten what you said, have you, Grandpa?"

"Me? Did I say something? What did I say?"

"The cookies."

"The cookies? Ah! the cookies!"

"Do you really think it's necessary?"

"You bet your life!"

He furtively slipped his hand into mine, and we were off.

As soon as we reached the house, as soon as we were plunged in the hard, white brightness of the courtyard after the cool dip of the shady vestibule, I caught a glimpse of the platter that awaited us on the doorstep to our room — a round platter with a cover over it and a round loaf of bread lying on top. We hadn't come back in time that day to receive our meal directly from Karima's hands.

"Run and set up the meïda. Quick," I whispered to Khelil in the profound drowsiness that always encompasses this house at mealtimes, the silence, all curtains drawn, it confines itself in."

I didn't have to ask twice. Setting the table is a chore my boy will readily, even enthusiastically, accomplish, especially since he just recently learned to roll ours across the floor like a hoop.

Karima. She's only a neighbor, but we're indebted to her for our physical sustenance. Ever since the day my daughter Adra died, she's provided us with our daily bread. In a way, she took Adra's place in our lives, and she did so without a lot of words or demonstrativeness, just sort of automatically. She's never forgotten us since. Providence evidently watches over the young woman, who has in turn become Providence for us.

It's very true that it's easier to give than to receive. But accepting what is offered to you is also an act of human charity. Take for example my daughter, lovely Adra as everyone used to call her, her husband hardly even waited for her to be buried before he disappeared, abandoning Khelil. Was I to refuse this child that destiny had bestowed upon me? It would have been a terrible mistake. It was the best thing that could have happened to me. I, who no longer had anyone, suddenly had someone — I had Khelil, this child who happens to be the living portrait of my daughter, who was herself the very image of my poor wife, Yamma, while she was still of this world, this boy upon whom I depend more than he does upon me.

I had to bend down in order to laboriously lift the large saucer-shaped platter with both hands: it was still hot. Then, having pushed the curtain to our room back with my elbow, I hurried to set it down on a meïda that had been set in just the right spot. In his eagerness, Khelil had forgotten neither the hand towel nor the pitcher of water.

Since then, I don't know how many days have passed — three, four? Their number makes no difference. During those days we never once reminisced about our visits to town — we'll be making our appearance again soon enough.

"Khelil, my boy, it's time we went out. Can you be ready soon?"

I spent these last few days closed up in the room.

"I'm coming, Grandpa."

"What's that child up to now?"

Every now and again, unexpectedly, I'm overcome with enormous sadness. It drags me into the deepest desolation, and my whole body aches so much that I take to my bed. There are certainly countless reasons for giving way to despair, but I have no idea what it is that gets me into that state on certain days.

"Khelil, are you coming now?"

It was undoubtedly because I'd thought about our well-wisher of the previous week again, and with one thing leading to another I'd suddenly realized: "He too must be pained by human suffering. But he had also prevented me from seeing his face! What wrong would there have been in that? I have no intention of getting angry with him over such a trifle, even less so for having taken me for a beggar. And if he decided in a glance that I was worthy of his generosity, then what was I to do about it? I've always done my utmost to remain respectable, dressing decently in summer as I do in winter. I know that I can in no way be counted among the ranks of miserable, anonymous creatures who roam about the streets of the city with outstretched hands. I am well-known, I was born into a good family, I'm not the sort of person one would ordinarily give charity to. But this fellow went and refused to let me see his face."

That's the way it had all begun, and when I ran out of arguments, it didn't take long for me to start wondering if it wouldn't be just as well for me to take my own life.

"Khelil, listen son, I have the feeling that we won't be going out today either, not yet."

"Oh, let's do go, Grandpa, please!" he implores.

And in a wee voice, he ventures, "Can I take my package of cookies?"

The same package that he'd been treasuring all this time without even opening.

"Of course. You can do whatever you like with it. It's yours!"

And with that, we leave the house.

*

The market looms into view. As usual, the crowd is thick as flies, and, suddenly, seeing the street that customarily led us to our observation post, I begin to feel uncomfortable. I can't explain what is happening to me or put into words the loathing that the thought of going back there, to the same spot, with the child inspires in me. No. Go and sit down on the doorstep of the shop that seems as though it will never again be opened. I can't.

I start down another street leading into it. I'm sure we'll find someplace else just as comfortable.

Then Khelil tugs at my arm so hard I almost stumble. Surprised, losing my temper, I scold, "What are you doing, you little brat? What is it?"

"You've taken a wrong turn!" he exclaims. "Can't you watch where you're going? This isn't the right way!"

Sizing him up with a severe look, I declare in a tone that leaves no room for discussion: "We're going to change places, for once. It won't hurt. On the contrary, we'll have a different view of things."

Stubbornly standing his ground two steps in front of me, he drinks me in with his bottomless eyes, eyes filled with incomprehension, doubt, and . . . reproach. Yes, that's exactly it, reproach. However, as I watch him, I'm not quite sure that he doesn't understand why we've taken another route instead of heading toward our favorite spot. "Ah well," I say to myself, "in that case, I won't have to explain it all to him." The longer he stares at me, the more I have the feeling he has understood, or is beginning to understand. Nevertheless, he doesn't seem to approve of my behavior. Standing planted there in the same place, he doesn't budge nor does he seem about to do so.

Trying to make up, I say, "Are you coming?"

I even go so far as to tease him, "Khelil, be careful. You'll end up taking root right there where you're standing!"

We have the good fortune of being able to understand each other without needing to speak. It's a blessing, but it turns to ill fortune at times and the blessing becomes a curse. I know what he's hoping for. He wants the miracle of the silver coin to be reproduced, and that's why his feet and his mind are frozen to the spot, refusing to go forward, to go anywhere else, meaning anywhere other than the place the first miracle occurred. Children are superstitious by nature.

As my little joke has no effect on him, I begin to grow impatient and say abruptly, "Come along now, will you?"

He remains standing there and continues to observe me with the same look on his face. Then, he silently hands me the package of cookies he had been hugging tightly under his arm. Only then do tears flood into his eyes, his lips contort and immediately purse into a scowl that makes me burn with shame and remorse.

And he even finds the strength to murmur, "I don't want them."

Just as I was preparing to be firm with him, I see myself from his eyes: grotesque. And so, without the slightest hesitation, I walk up to him, take him by the hand, and we walk away in the direction of our regular place, the place where we always sit.

Why not, after all? That doorstep is as familiar with us as we are with it, and besides, the view of the covered market we have from there is like a friendly face.

*

Having barely sat down at my side, Khelil begins fidgeting with his package. I enjoy watching out of the corner of my eye how, with a

trembling hand, he painstakingly struggles to open it without ripping the paper, how afterwards his fingers forage about inside and
finally pull out a cake, which he gravely offers me.

"It's for you, Grandpa."

"Come now, Khelil, are you joking? Cookies at my age! Don't be
silly! Keep them for yourself."

"Please, Grandpa."

I accept the little round cake.

Sitting there on our step, nibbling at those sweet treats, we observe the familiar movements of the crowd whose instincts and behavior patterns remain unaltered, going round in circles as if it
were turning around the Kaaba, circling until it made one dizzy,
yet we can't take our eyes off the scene.

Suddenly, it's as if, in place of the covered market, a sumptuous
palace materializes. I admire the grand double staircase leading up
to the first floor; my innermost desire is to climb those stairs, get a
glimpse of the rooms, the galleries, and all the marvelous secrets
that are hidden up there. At the same time, I feel that I'm probably
still lucid enough to realize I've never been up those stairs in my
whole, long life — I mean to say, the stairs of our covered market.
Just then, the loud-speakers — yes, them again — let loose and,
rumbling, roaring, obliterating all other sounds, launch into their
call to prayer. I have to shout in order to inform Khelil: "It's time to
go! We have to go home now!"

"What?" he asks, screwing up his face like a deaf person.

Repeating, even louder, I bellow at him, "Home! Home!"

Then he, in the same earth-shaking voice, "But the man didn't
come by yet!"

"What man?"

The loudspeakers grow quiet. The silence that follows leaves us
deafened, but slowly, from that stillness, the hubbub resuscitates
in small geysers bubbling up, and the throngs in the marketplace
come back to life, shake themselves from their stupor.

As if he hadn't noticed anything, Khelil howls again at the top of his voice: "The man who is going to give us another coin!"

"Quiet, boy! Don't shout so loudly! The man who . . . Why that's preposterous! Have you lost your senses? It's time to go home now!"

"Then you won't be able to buy any tobacco!"

And again, moaning at the top of his lungs: "You won't be able to smoke!"

The thundering loudspeakers had caused quite a bit of damage. The people were dispersed, their ranks had considerably thinned out. Khelil and I found ourselves among the last stragglers in the marketplace.

"I won't be able to smoke? But it doesn't matter, son. I don't need to smoke."

I think it over for a few minutes and promise: "We'll come back tomorrow."

"Oh, all right then," he says.

Smoking.

Back then, in the mountains, smoking. It was so very, very long ago that at times I ask myself: "When was that? In some other world, some other life?" We had been lying in ambush for the French soldiers, but we were the ones who fell into the hands of one of their platoons. Our whole group was taken prisoner. First, they interrogated us — one at a time — then herded us into a fenced-in area. Hours went by. I didn't keep track of them. I no longer had a watch. In any case, time seemed to have stopped, crushed under the weight of the cascade of heat spilling down from the blazing sun in which we, the captives, were roasting, left out in full exposure. Condensing, growing heavy, time itself seemed to have congealed. I was clinging to the chain-link fence, thinking only of keeping my eyes open and, if humanly possible, fixing my gaze beyond that compound. I concentrated so hard on it that I forgot to wonder about afterwards, about what was going to happen to us. But it had been chance that brought us there, and chance would just have to come up with its own solutions.

Just then one of those French soldiers came up to me, all red-cheeked, his blond hair cropped short, just a kid, and, through the fence, he slipped a lit cigarette between my fingers. It had happened in exactly the same way that the stranger had placed the coin in my palm several days ago. Exactly the same way. And in the same way, I barely got a glimpse of that soldier's face, who still looked like a schoolboy, for he had turned his back immediately. What ever became of him? I'm still alive. But is he?

"All right, we'll come back tomorrow," says my little Khelil. "And I'll bet you anything that the nice man comes back too."

When a world can no longer remedy its own ills, it's very hard to help it become a fair place to live again — even after having gone up into the mountains to die and then ending up coming back down again. That's what life today is all about.

Hand in hand, Khelil and I walk off toward home. After a few moments, I feel as though we are being escorted by a host of specters. I know the feeling and I'm also familiar with the physical nearness that spirits, sometimes even more skillfully than living beings, can make one feel when they get it into their minds to envelop us in their presence — be it a young soldier having come up to me with a cigarette almost thirty years ago now and, though he may be alive today, living somewhere else, there's nothing to prevent him from still being here; be it my fallen comrades, knowing why they are fallen, out there in the maquis, or keeping them company; or a certain Adra; or a certain Yamma — they never abandon us, even in this raging autumn sunshine. And if I sometimes think they have, deserted us that is, it can only be an oversight on my part, the result of my senses growing dull. They never leave us. Sometimes I hear them laughing behind my back and then other times crying.

And it just so happens as we are walking toward the house I sink into a deep silence, listening intently: *who knows, one of them just might feel like laughing, or crying.*

My hopes are dashed, but that's understandable — they always just do whatever they please.

So may the bells sound out the day of reckoning. Let them ring loudly in this pure, blue sky, and we shall all be reunited.

"Grandpa," Khelil asks worriedly, "the man will come back, won't he? He'll come back again, isn't that so?"

"Yes, of course. He'll come back."

Butterflies

Screaming: "Kill! Kill!"

It started up again: "Kill! Kill!"

Was it someone? Or something else entirely? He was running. That's all he was doing: just running. Running from one street to the next in his Dobrinja neighborhood, but he didn't recognize them, those streets looking stranger and stranger, streets that he knew like the back of his hand, and he didn't recognize them, and he was running. They were so gray, so empty. He was running. It wasn't really night, nor was it day. At times silhouettes went slipping after each other down at the end of one of the streets but only to take refuge in some entryway or wherever they could. But he was running to catch one of them, attack it with his rifle, an AK47 whose weight he no longer felt as he bore it in his all too frail, too feeble arms. And the streets he was running through were all desperately empty, unrecognizably empty, while that voice kept screaming: "Kill! Kill!"

It was screaming somewhere — maybe it was screaming inside his head and he was spitting. He was spitting up his lungs, spitting up his stomach and everything in it. Spitting to the right and to the left and running the whole time. With the urge to vomit tightening in his throat, he could sense that silence, that grayness closing in on him. He pushed in on his stomach with his free arm. He was still choking it back. Then suddenly, like vomiting, he screamed out: "Kill! Kill!"

What was it waiting for, that other realm all around out there, why didn't it say something to him, answer him! That's what he, Izet, was waiting for. He stopped running after having screamed. And what if he got an answer? What would he do then? Eyes and ears peeled, straining into the dim silence. So many windows, so many doors. If, from one of them, something — what? Ominous windows, ominous doors, all closed. But what if the first one just happened to open? Or merely crack open — crack open and what? Maybe some black look would spring from it, or a black bullet, something else just as black that would come running out into the streets screaming, "Kill! Kill!" Screaming, running after you then chasing you all the way out there into the countryside. But still closed, the doors, windows, and death were waiting.

And it came again: "Kill!"

"Izet, Izet, my sweet, wake up! I'm here, Mama's here with you."

Twisting in his sleep, stronger than his mother, the child grabbed her, thrashed about. Nightmares, if you had managed to escape the bombs and the machine-gun fire. That was still the price to pay, nights. And days you went around bleary-eyed, with circles under them just as dark as at night. You only survived from one hour to the next to be miserable in your misery.

Finally, Najla got a grip on her son's wrists, pinned them across his chest. Izet calmed down, his legs, relaxed now, stretched out, his breathing became hushed. Suddenly, he was sleeping peacefully.

The mother sat looking at the body, already grown so big, that seemed to be floating on a bed of water and then, she didn't know why, she hurried to pick him up, to hug him close to her breast. Settling him down afterwards on her knees, she began to rock him. Then she wept.

Izet fixed her with one of those childish looks that takes everything in, that appears to understand everything human and everything inhuman as well. Unblinkingly, he observed the mother's tears, tears we all find so natural. He watched her in that way for several minutes before Najla noticed. And noticing, she was at a loss for words. She gave him a poor, wet smile.

Lately, for no apparent reason, he could get a look in his eyes that would leave her bewildered, helpless. Under his high rounded forehead, fringed with rebel curls, her eyes would plunge into their deep azure only to discover strange abysses. That immutable blue was obviously all-knowing, was plainly well-versed in all things as well as in the tragedy that had befallen them, and yet never did a cloud darken their blue purity. It was the same for the resolute, firm little chin with its dimple — never had a fear made it tremble.

He remained quietly there in her arms, so very quiet that, observing him through her tears, she finally convinced herself that he was still sleeping, sheltered under the clear sky of his eyes.

In fact, he had decided upon this himself: don't show the slightest sign of life, just study the mother's face, the icy whiteness framed with a shawl, a sign of mourning to be kept on even at home and in the height of summer, study the two tiny folds of suffering dug into either side of the mouth, sound out the drowned horizon of those eyes — eyes that for three days now, ever since that terrifying morning, seemed to have faded to the point of extinction. He was trying to understand what it was like to be a woman who had been raped.

*

Three days ago, he was coming home from having fetched the water when he found her sprawled on the bare floor. He'll never be able to forget seeing her sitting in that position, legs spread apart, breasts exposed, her clothing torn to shreds, and that look — what a look — that empty, glassy look of the dead people along the way to the fountain, the people shot down from up in the hills by the Tchetniks for having come, like himself, to get their supply of water. What his mother had been through hadn't been at all difficult for him to figure out. It was the same ones; they had done to her what they did to Muslim women. Other Muslim women had already been their victims — his two cousins, Tima and Zuhra, and some friends, Sena, Zerina, Enisa . . . And Izet knew that just as well as anyone else did.

He had immediately dropped his brimming jerrican in the entryway, turned round, and run to the stairs of the building. He had seen them coming down when he'd walked in: there were four of them. Armed and in combat clothing. Four. Just as he was passing them, he'd been seized with inexplicable apprehension. The bastards!

He wasn't even aware of how he had torn down the flights of stairs in a flash and run out into the avenue. Instinctively, he knew which way to go. Without hesitating, he struck out at a gallop, his heart nearly bursting. And then he caught sight of them, up there ahead of him with their backs turned. They looked so like hardened soldiers, he knew it was them; he would have recognized them blindfolded.

He did, however, have to stop, wait for a twisting pain in his side to pass. He didn't have to run so hard anymore, he wouldn't lose sight of them now, oh no. He followed along at the same regular pace they set, and like an impavid machine ticking along, his only thought was to tail them.

The café-bar on Partizanske Olimpijade Street. They went inside. Then he reached it in turn, but stopping on the threshold, he posted himself against one of the double glass doors. They had already sat down at a table, and the first one he was able to identify was a tenant in their building, the Serb, Zivan. The thick lower lip, his close-set, glaucous eyes almost touched at the base of his nose: an ugly character. Though they were familiar to him, Izet couldn't pin a name on the three other faces. They must surely live in his neighborhood. He promised himself to check into it. Their image burned itself into his memory.

There were many of their kind sitting at neighboring tables, some of them with rifles leaning against their legs. Afraid of being recognized by Zivan, Izet backed slowly away until he was out of sight.

*

In the city, you would run into dead people sitting up in live positions. When he had come back home, he found his mother hadn't moved. Without wasting a minute, he went to find a towel in the linen closet. Using the water he had brought home, he wet it and silently began to wipe off his mother's face, then her neck, then her chest. He finished up with her legs and pulled the skirt back down over them. Next, he took off the blouse, the brassiere — both in shreds — and with gentle movements replaced them for her with much prettier ones. With that done, slipping his hand under her arm, he urged her to get up. She gave him a grateful look, which moved Izet, shed some tears, which he hadn't wanted, against which he steeled himself, rebelled. They shook his heart, but not him, really.

It was enough that his mother in coming back to her senses came back to him as well. As he helped her, he could see her pushing herself off the floor, then getting to her feet. He led her over toward the divan, where he sat her down while he huddled himself up at her feet and wrapped both arms around her legs.

Did they spend a long or just a short time together in that way? It hardly mattered. Time didn't matter to anyone now, no one bothered about it anymore. Time. Under the watchful eye of death, you don't count the minutes or the hours anymore, the days become eternally empty. But you could talk, and if you wanted to, you could even remain completely silent.

*

"Mama, why are they doing this? Why are they doing this to us?"

Words, after a long time, that cropped up all by themselves as if dreamed aloud, said in a voice that didn't really expect an answer.

And yet it came, the answer, but such a long time afterwards, "I don't know, Izet."

Those curious little-girl inflections. You could sense some nameless fear in them. If his mother kept on in that horrible voice, Izet was going to knock his head up against the walls of the room. Waiting, he strained to listen.

She continued, less imploring than enjoining him, "And don't you try to find out either."

The same unavowed terror.

"Please. Nothing ever happened. Izet, you don't know anything."

"But it did happen," thought the child. "It really did happen. What will become of us now?"

"They won't stop, Mama! They've done it to other women! Even to little girls! They'll make others live through what you have!"

"Be quiet, Izet. Be quiet."

That wan voice — it sounded as though it were coming from the other side of the world, running up from the very depths of horror.

And his mother added, "I want to die, Izet."

A sick woman, exhausted from suffering, who just couldn't take any more, that was what she had become now.

"Mama!"

"Don't say anything, Izet. Don't say anything more, please."

Silence fell again and, like dead ash, buried everything in the room — the plain furniture, the oriental vases that came from the copper bazaar, the Koranic calligraphies in their frames, the television set — objects that soon seemed to be molded from ash themselves and that the first breath of wind to crack the white heat of this July day would not easily disperse.

Holding one another tightly, the mother and the child found no more words to share: were they listening to the heavy, ramming blows that the Serb artillery was firing off in the distance? Screams, faint cries, motors furiously fulminating, horns bleating — noises rumbling in on the night, bringing with them the sound of the city breathing intently, clinging desperately to life. And they, abandoned by all, the father off fighting somewhere but abandoning them nevertheless, so close to one another they could forget each other's presence, they were listening.

Pulling away from his mother, his voice high pitched, a host of memories suddenly flooding back to him, Izet began again, "At the Smajlovics, they even killed the baby. You knew that baby, she brought him here one day, Mama. Her name was Samira, and his was Samir. You thought he was so cute, I remember."

"That's enough! Be quiet."

"And now, he's dead."

Breathing heavily, Najla sighed, "Bring me something to drink instead."

The boy jumped to his feet, went to get some water directly from the jerrican and came back and stood before her holding out the glass. He couldn't keep himself from asking one more time, he just couldn't help it, "I would just like to know, when they do that, why do they do it, Mama."

Najla, shaking her head, was attempting to sob without being able to. She soon choked on the water she was drinking and was seized with a fit of coughing. Izet took the glass from her hands and patted her on the back; better yet: he leaned against her, caressed her. However, not changing the subject of conversation, he made a fresh attempt.

"The baby looked like he was sleeping, except that he wasn't in his bed, and he was dead. They were all looking at him, the people who had come there just to see that, and no one dared pick him up, go and bloody their hands just to lay him in his mother's arms, who was dead too, even though her eyes were open, just like his were. It was funny. They both seemed to be sleeping, even with their eyes open, except that he — the baby — looked like he had peed, but it was just blood. We were pretty near them. We were looking at them and we were still afraid to get just a bit closer and do something for them. I wonder why. Because even with their eyes open they seemed to be asleep, and we didn't? Nobody could blame us — we've seen so many people die, haven't we Mama?"

Totally absorbed in his story, paying no attention to his mother, surprised that she had let him speak his piece, the boy glanced over at her. She was sitting there, silently rocking back and forth. He suddenly understood. It was his talking about such frightful and yet such commonplace things: that's what was doing this to her. His mother was losing her mind; his throat suddenly clutched with spasms. But if he just stopped talking, wouldn't the silence that would come sweeping down upon them be even more unbearable? And already, in that silence, they could both hear the sounds of their own tragedy, of their own suffering, mingled with the exploding shells, with the sound of the whole city being crushed underfoot by a relentless beast.

As if in apology, Izet made an announcement that was nevertheless quite important, "They're distributing packages today, Mama. I have to go."

"No, don't go. Please, don't go. No, Izet, stay here."

Words in the throat suddenly weeping for the eyes, in place of them, for the source of tears had gone dry, weeping, trying to say something else without being able to find the words, the real ones, the only words, without being able to do anything else, not even console someone, even Izet, and even less comfort the man who was fighting for them — but where: up there in the mountains? That place deep inside of you that can do nothing more than simply let these dry tears speak.

"Now Mama, there's nothing left to eat. Nothing left of anything."

And the mother, with that infrangible premonition of disaster still in her voice, "That's just too bad. Too bad. We should be damned for expecting benevolent strangers to feed us, to come to our aid."

"I have to go. I must go, we can't miss this."

Izet brushed back the fine golden coils flowing down on either side of the mother's face with his two hands, made them go back into place under the shawl, smoothed them down so they would stay there, and, as though he were speaking to a little girl, reassured her.

"I won't be long. Do you hear? I won't be long, you'll see."

Before Najla could say another word, he had disappeared.

*

Pushing through the door, arms stretched around a large cardboard box sealed with bands of tape, Izet, back already, burst into the apartment. He hadn't taken long to get back, that was true. Under the golden skin, his face was flushed as much with the sweltering heat as with excitement. He was beaming mutely and hadn't yet set down his load when, from the doorway, his eyes darted to his mother. Stretched out on the divan, breath suspended, she was sleeping without really seeming to be. The child went pale. "She's not breathing." With the heavy box still in his arms he drew nearer, he could sense a hint of breath, hovering about his mother rather than emanating from her. Then, he too breathed in relief, and gazing upon her, upon the fragile and fearsome self-forgetfulness in which she seemed to have sought refuge and renounced the world, he was very tempted to awaken her, almost did, so he could show her his loot, so she'd be proud of him. A second more, and he would have. Then he backed away, spurred by a feeling of profanation. He crept quietly off to put down the package that had been growing heavier in his arms all the time. Heaving it onto the table, he began immediately, feverishly ripping off the tape. Feverishly, but trying not to make more noise than necessary.

And the box revealed its treasures: colorful canned goods, jars with marvelous labels, cellophane sacks with he knew not what inside — all of it delightful, magical. After having quickly discovered what could only be chocolate, two enormous bars like two surfboards, his heart began beating so fast that it hurt. He took care not to cry out with joy, but thankful tears welled into his eyes.

His hands, rummaging around in the package, touching, feeling this and that, suddenly abandoned their task. They were now lying inert on the edges of the box. Without realizing it, Izet was lost deep in thought, contemplating this manna sent from heaven. His eyes were staring fixedly out beyond the walls of the room, beyond the walls of the building, off into the distance.

Yet it didn't take him long to come back to his senses and, with the furtive gestures of a thief, stealthily grab the bars of chocolate, slip them under his shirt, and, still like a thief, making no sound, vanish, but not without carrying the image of his sleeping mother, which he took in with a glance, along with him.

*

He didn't come back this time for quite a long while, and in place of the chocolate bars, some strange sort of balls were sticking out under the material of his shirt, as if three or four breasts had somehow grown on his stomach. Najla, whom he found awake, standing with her back turned, was busily emptying the food from the box; she had already set some of it out on the table as if for a display. Izet instinctively crossed his arms over his secret.

"Look at it all, Mama! It came from America. And you didn't want me to go. We've never been spoiled like this before."

He got a real kick out of teasing his mother once in a while.

"They can afford to spoil us! Considering the price we have to pay. But where did you go off to again?"

"To see if I could find some new butterflies for my collection."

"Izet, Izet, with everything that's going on around us! You'll drive me crazy."

These worries of hers caused a thought to echo in the child's mind, a thought that was very consoling in a way: "After what they've done to her, she seems to be feeling as good as any woman can these days." Her back remained turned while she was talking. Izet took the opportunity to sneak into the next room where his bed was with a row of books at its head, his books. Back in there, safely tucked away, he stashed the four offensive grenades that he had obtained in exchange for the chocolate.

*

Rather than in the cemetery, the dead made their bed almost anywhere in the city. No place was off-limits to them — squares, public gardens, parks were their territory. When it came to butterflies, this state of affairs was just fine with Izet. He would have been the last to complain. With these thousand and one graves — all laid with flowers, even the most humble — there had never been such an invasion of butterflies. But, come to think of it, in times when people hadn't enough bread to eat, where did this profusion of bouquets, of wreaths come from? Oddly enough, it didn't surprise anyone. No one ever asked about it, and as far as Izet was concerned, it would have been indecent to ask, the only important question being whether or not you could feel just a little bit happy about anything. And for him, it was the butterflies that filled him with happiness. He was crazy about them.

Sure, he collected them, but that was a pretext — it was simply his way of justifying his love for them. Just watching them, alive, flying along their unpredictable course, fancy-free, whimsical, dancing, made him feel so utterly ecstatic, he experienced true moments of grace. A polychromatic fairyland, a dream dreamed with open eyes that told of a lost Eden, a thought that in the very same instant and in that same unpredictable, fancy-free, whimsical, dancing way would have taken off for the paradise that Izet would have recognized anywhere — that's what butterflies were. The spirits of flowers, the sighs of the soul, the inspirations of angels.

And so he could never bring himself to capture one lightheartedly, be it the most beautiful, the most dazzling without at least having run after it, coming and going interminably and giving it every chance. Even then, it was most often only a game. Izet would end up abandoning the chase and sparing the creature's life and liberty. It would immediately be off carrying the message he had entrusted in it. It would be off, and even then he would follow its flight for as long as it stayed in view, however unpredictable, fancy-free, whimsical, dancing was its path. Even then, even after it had disappeared, he still followed its ghost with his eyes. It was carrying the precious message to the world, sent by him and also by the dead, who with all their flowers took up more space in the city than the living and who therefore remained human. It was the butterfly's duty to make their dream last, to ensure that it would be nurtured, answered humanly.

*

Izet, sitting on a step, his chin in his hands, waited patiently in the stairwell of the building. Zivan would come home all right, sooner or later, the day was drawing to an end. The shadows that met you here were cool on your skin for a little while, then it passed — the sense of well-being was over, and the crushing heat would overwhelm you again.

Every single minute of the morning and of the afternoon for the last few days, Izet had spied on him, had tailed him, had watched his every movement. Methodical, Zivan, accompanied by his three acolytes — always the same ones — would go to the place he had planned to carry out his filthy task and afterwards, in conformance with some strange rite, he would drag his accomplices to the café-bar in Partizanske Olimpijade Street. There, in silence, they would empty drink after drink.

Unfortunately, while he was waiting for him in the half-light of the stairwell, Izet would often see other tenants of the building, or strangers — always someone coming in at the same time as Zivan. With his ugly mug, his burned-out eyes, the brute would come up along with the others, nearly bumping into Izet each time he went by and cursing in a thick voice. In the end, he would go into his apartment. Nothing would happen.

But the boy didn't give up hope. One evening Zivan would finally come through the front door of the building alone.

And that evening came at last. With a start, Izet stood up at the same time and, with every muscle in his body taught, coiled like springs, watched the man who was beginning to come up the stairs — and no one in the stairwell, still no one.

The child, one flight above, leaned his chest against the railing. He called out, "Here, Zivan, it's for you!"

Down below the man instinctively held out his hands, caught the grenade that had been thrown to him. Izet tore himself away from where he'd been standing, ran up the stairs.

He was already at home when he felt the explosion rock their building.

*

"During the day, a fiery monster comes to stand before the city. It waits for night to fall and then devours part of the town."

"It's time to go to sleep now, Mama."

"We are constantly living our last minutes, Izet, so let's not spend them sleeping."

The absolute silence spit and crackled in the night, the night that the monster had locked around them, the night, all the nights, in which that monster lurked.

Najla hadn't said another word. She was undoubtedly sleeping now, as Izet had begged her to do. And then suddenly: "We shed our clothing when we enter the water. We should also drop our thoughts, the words with which we all drape ourselves, before slipping away into sleep. But of course with clothing it's simple. How might we do it with our thoughts?"

Izet, eyes opened wide in the darkness, was telling himself: "I don't want to look forward or backward but just right at the place I'm in now and try to see if I can get out of this alive. With my mother, if possible."

And also: "There wasn't much left to put into Zivan's casket and, therefore, no soul to be reborn in the blessed flight of butterflies."

"Did you hear that, Izet? A bombing."

"No, Mother."

"Yes, there it is again."

"It's probably only a building that just finished falling down."

"On its tenants?"

"Of course not."

"Oh, Izet, Izet, how can you be so sure?"

"Because I know."

"One thing you don't know: they're going to end up smashing in the whole world, then they'll smash in the clouds, and after that, they'll smash in the sky."

"Go to sleep, Mama. You don't have to worry about that."

"I don't have to worry about that!"

Once again, that silence spread out, not a dazed silence, but always keenly alert. This once, it lasted for so long that the boy imagined his mother drifting peacefully far, very far away from this unhappy place.

And yet she broke through the great expanse of darkness, of emptiness, and came back with dreamy words so sweet, almost childlike, she took on form.

"It's like a war film, but with us in it and in which everything is real. Don't you think so, Izet?"

"Yes, that's what it's like."

"I'm going to teach you, son, what this war is about, why it's different from others. It's because we live in a world in which everyone wants to have the last word."

"That may be so, Mama. Go to sleep now, rest a little."

"And while we're sleeping, the monster will finish devouring the town."

"There is no monster, there are only people killing each other."

"Bear in mind, my boy, that you can't outrun your shadow or your own death either."

"Come on, Mama, why are you talking like this?"

*

During the next few days, in addition to the machine-gunning, the pounding of mortar shells, three separate explosions each made one of the other buildings in the neighborhood rock on its foundations, and each time it was exactly the same: the explosions took place in a stairwell. But with everything else you had to deal with, what more could you say? You'd barely begun to talk about it when a new disaster cropped up, creating a diversion. So you just lumped it in with all the rest, and it didn't change anything, didn't add anything to the sum of horrors that you, and everyone else, had already had your fill of. Then there was also the insoluble problem that kept cropping back up, the daily obsession: survival. Run around after bread, water, candles, lamp oil, an egg, firewood. Instead of finding one of these things, you had a good chance of meeting your death but, since you had no choice, you would go anyway.

One day Izet had seen several of their neighbors go down with axes and kill the only tree growing in front of their building. It was a plane tree, he was sure of that, a tree that peeled and scattered the pieces of its patchwork trunk into the street — some spinach-green, others light or brownish-green, still others almost white. They had cut up the tree and shared out the parts, which they'd hurriedly carried away, and this strange thing happened almost immediately afterwards: the birds. Those birds that had come flying over and then back over, knowing there was a certain tree in that spot — a tree in which to seek refuge from the bombs. They had circled, wheeled, and, beating the air with their wings, apparently totally confused, had flown away as swiftly as possible.

Death. Even so, you still had to have a moment's respite to think about it.

*

Explosions, identical in every aspect, there had been four of them. After each one, Izet came home, eyes crazed, only to slam his back up against the closed door of their apartment and stay rooted to the spot. A statue, his arms glued to his sides, his shoulders hunched up, his face chalk-colored, his mouth open, a statue that wasn't breathing.

At first, shocked to find him looking so unreal, Najla hadn't dared to go to him. Frightened, she observed him from a distance, trying with all her might, yet in vain, trembling from head to foot until it finally overwhelmed her, and, like a sleep-walker, with dazed steps, she threw herself forward, grabbed him, covered his head with her arms, hugged him against her, hugged him to her breast.

Izet would then smother those words in the flesh that had born him, invariably the same words, "It isn't right to kill people, is it, Mama?"

Letter to Mother

Finally, he broke down and demanded, "How could you have ever married that man, Mother?"

The question dumbfounded Mme. Weiser, whose radiant beauty defied the wholesome mounds of pinkish flesh that had been conferred upon her by the ripe age of fifty and that were quite skillfully fitted into the deep blue Chanel suit, a blue which matched her eyes exactly and seemed to go naturally with her golden complexion.

"Are you speaking of your father, David?"

"My father, my father!"

The sarcasm with which the boy had pronounced the word *father* would have made you think that he might go on indefinitely in that scathing and ironic tone of voice. But no, that's not what he did. He stopped right there, sullen and tortured with unvented anger.

Judging from the look on her face, Mme. Weiser didn't understand what her son was talking about or what he was getting at in the least.

"What is it, David, what's wrong?"

The young man didn't answer. Actually, he seemed to have nothing more to say, and they just stood there facing one another in silence.

Mme. Weiser slowly became conscious of this standoff. She gave him a gentle, amused smile, the type of smile that a mother allows herself to use on such occasions, a smile that not only lit up her face but buoyed her whole being. He turned away, glowering, sad-eyed. Then, just as she did every time they caught her attention, Mme. Weiser thought, "Good Lord, what magnificent eyes!"

Yet today she didn't recognize her son — didn't recognize that face or its expression, the stubborn, impregnable expression and features. She couldn't read him like a book as she usually did.

She was still lit up with that same loving smile, that same compassion for human beings, when she asked again gravely, "What do you hold against him? Don't forget he's your father and he always will be. Even though there are irritating things about him, he's no different than we are."

"He's not one of us! He's not a member of our family."

The rejection came as a heavy blow. Mme. Weiser's smile didn't really fade, it grew twisted. "Why not, Dave? Please explain what you mean."

"He's a stranger, Mother, a stranger."

"Not at all. He's Jewish too. Just like you and I are."

"No, Mother, we're Jews from the death camps! He isn't."

Mme. Weiser's handsome face changed color this time. She was seized with an uncontrollable fit of hiccups, and a cold glimmer of folly suddenly flared in her eyes. There was no mistaking it — she was laughing, but only because her son had to be made to feel utterly ridiculous.

"How dare you say that about your father? You simply have no idea what you're talking about. You weren't even born back in those days. You couldn't have been, I only married three years after I got back from . . . *over there!*"

She repeated, "Three years afterwards, David. You weren't born yet. How can you talk about the death camps?"

"So it seems to you, Mother. So it seems. That's what you believe. I, too, was *over there.* You didn't know it, but I was there too. I was there! I was there! I was there!"

The sobs that shook David's body were every bit as violent and painful as his words. He held them back, gulped them back down.

Mme. Weiser cupped her hands around the boy's face.

He calmed down.

The mother's face also regained its composure.

*

156

Mme. Weiser had knocked at David's door using the code they had decided on together — two quick raps, then two more, farther apart — and nothing, no answer. Yet she knew he was in there. And so she began again with two quick raps and then two more, farther apart. Still nothing — the door remained a closed wooden face.

Mme. Weiser was not one to be so easily discouraged. Without knocking again, she stood posted, forcing herself to be patient. Patience was nothing new to her — it was something that had been necessary to learn *over there*.

At least three or four minutes went by, and without a sign of warning, without a single noise that might have given him away, David's voice unexpectedly spoke out on the other side of the door — a voice that suddenly seemed so close to Mme. Weiser that it made her shudder, and if she hadn't made such a habit of self control, she would certainly have pulled back with a start.

"What is it, Mother?"

He must have been speaking to her with his mouth right up against the wood panel of the door. And though the words were soft, muffled, they were nevertheless intelligible, and murmuring, as he had decided to do for fun, was still enough to make himself heard.

"So, what is it, Mother?"

"I'm the one who should be asking you that question. Why did you take all the furniture out of your room? If you have a good reason, I would certainly like to hear it. Go ahead, son."

A long, drawn-out silence was all that came from the other side. But deep, mellow laughter soon followed. And David's voice rang out, still very near, "Did you have any furniture, Mother, in the death camp? Did you have a comfortable setup *over there?*

The voice fell silent for a few minutes, and then, "Would you have thought of such things as furniture? Weren't there much more urgent things, much more urgent things?"

In a clear voice, Mme. Weiser answered, "Yes, Dave, there were more urgent things."

Pensively, with her head slightly bowed, probably from the sheer weight of concentration, she stood listening. It was difficult to say what she was expecting from the door that was more and yet less than a door — a door that separated them and yet brought them together at the same time. Frontier or Ark of the Covenant, it could not be blamed for existing and doing what it was meant to do simply because it existed.

Mme. Weiser waited a few more minutes. Her son's voice could no longer be heard. She walked away without saying anything else. In retreating, she had to make her way around David's furniture, piled high in the large entryway.

*

Sitting there on the bare floor, hunched down into one corner of the room, knees pulled up against his chest and his head leaning back against the wall, David was wrapped in a brown blanket. He seemed to be dozing, and perhaps he truly was asleep. His eyes were closed. At any rate, he was wearing that mask of sleep in which a trapped smile can sometimes make a face seem even stranger to the world.

His father glanced around the room that was bare of all furniture, of all objects. "Cleaned out," he said to himself, "so it will be a place only by default, with no particular characteristics." And, as if to better examine it, as if to better define the emptiness, the vacancy, he lifted his glasses to his eyes.

With her hands flat against either side of her face, Mme. Weiser only had eyes for David, David huddled up in his corner. Horrified, she wondered if he was sleeping, if she should trust appearances. Something convinced her not to. Nevertheless, without being aware of it, she managed to keep herself from breathing. Was it because of what she saw there, because of the faint stench floating in the air? And where might that smell be coming from, the stench of unkempt, decrepit bodies? Faint, yet suffocating, that same smell of mass graves and disinfectant from *over there*. From *over there* that smell was catching up with her here. The smell of everything she had known *over there* was coming back to her, rushing into her memory. It was like the barbed wire strung at different levels all around them, but it wasn't really barbed wire, only an imitation, and yet drawn on the walls so skillfully — replicated in such minute detail by David's hand, Mme. Weiser concluded, recalling that one day he had asked for a box of paints, a request that had quite surprised her, but everyone in the household was so quick to fulfill the boy's every wish. There was no doubt about it, the illusion was perfect to the point of actually fooling you. And even better, strung taut as the barbed wire seemed to be, it created another illusion, that of the space beyond, uninhabitable, a horizon devoid of birds or trees, a horizon that could never have inspired a dream.

Simultaneously, yet without consulting one another, M. and Mme. Weiser backed away, slipped quietly out of the room. M. Weiser was still holding his glasses absent-mindedly in one hand.

Then David opened his eyes, those incredibly transparent eyes of his, eyes in which the world had simply faded away.

Leaning his cheek against the wall: *I've walked so far, been through so many seasons, months, days, without keeping track of them, to reach the gates to the city of the last gathering place — I should already be upon its ramparts by now. I've been able to see the city in all of its glory, way off in the distance, for such a long time now, and I still haven't arrived. Will I ever get there? A voice whispers in my ear: "You aren't the only one to have undertaken the journey, and you won't be the last to be admitted. Keep on walking, continue along your path. Soon, you may rest. You have already crossed the entire desert."*

*

Now David's face seemed ageless, and his expression was that of someone whose entire attention was turned inward, thinking only of — of what, what reality? Of the shadow that can no longer find the person who is casting it?

He no longer considered his room off limits, and if the door had set certain limits of its own, that was its prerogative. It was none of his business — it mattered as little to him as when it would swing half-way open at certain times of the day to let in the servant carrying his meal tray. And even that food, a gruel so thin that it looked like nothing more than murky water, he could very well have done without. In any case, he had refused to accept anything else for a long time now.

Upon entering his room, Mme. Weiser found her son standing barefoot, facing the wall. All things considered, the position didn't terribly surprise her. Not in the light of recent events! What did shake her, on the other hand, was seeing his pajamas — striped up and down with vertical bars that could only have been the result of his own handiwork — those pajamas that he never took off anymore.

At the sight of the pajamas, Mme. Weiser had clenched her jaw, and finding herself incapable of relaxing it, she hissed between her closed teeth, "What have you done, my boy?"

The answer was a question put to the wall, "Done what?"

"Your pajamas, David."

"I've arrived at my destination. I'm waiting for the end now."

He suddenly turned around, contemplated her. She saw a pale, curdled twilight contemplating her, contemplating her ample curves buttoned into the deep blue suit. That body had escaped the crematory furnaces by what miracle? And that was all he thought. His mind ran up against impenetrably obscure places, which even the light of a thousand suns could never breach, the unthinkable, that which his mother had escaped. This being was his mother, and he didn't understand what miracle had kept her safe for him nor what other miracle had allowed her to keep him safe, shelter him too, for he knew full well that somewhere furnaces would soon be ready to be lit once again.

"I'm waiting to be gassed, Mother. Gassed and then incinerated. The burned body that I'll turn into then won't be me anymore, but I must be burned in order to become something other than this pitiful body."

David was looking through his mother as if through an open

door, and he saw: *My head on one of the gates to the city where we will gather. I will soon be able to rest my head. For such a long time, every step I took was filled with anxiety, and now it's over with, or it soon will be. I'm going towards it now, but it could be coming toward me as well. That thought warms my heart, just as those walls that I can see off in the distance are a welcome sight. I'll soon be making my entrance and I will have at last found peace. Keep on walking. One more step. And then another. Please legs, don't abandon me now, hold me up. Don't let my strength betray me. Just one last effort. I've been lucky up to now, but soon I'll be even luckier.*

*

"David, you probably aren't aware of it, but I might remind you that classes will be beginning soon at the university. Don't you think you should be preparing yourself for them?"

From his squatting position, the boy craned his neck. His eyes, with a far-away, very far-away, look, found his mother.

He answered, only after a long pause, in a stony voice, "Mother, how can *you* talk to me about the university and classes when I'm here, in a death camp, at the entrance to the gas chamber? How can you?"

"And you, David, why are you making yourself unhappy for no reason and making us all unhappy as well?"

"Forgive me, Mother?"

After that hushed question, the young man retreated into his silence.

He seemed to have said everything he wanted to say, and the way he just sat crouching there, and would probably continue to do so, with a glassy-eyed expression on his face, made it fairly obvious that he wouldn't say another word.

He did continue, but from then on it was in a nearly voiceless whisper, "You were spared, Mother. But I, I will not be."

Mme. Weiser wished that she could take refuge in tears, but since her return from the camps, she hadn't been able to muster them anymore. Her eyes remained dry.

Undoubtedly because he saw her just standing there, not moving, David went on in the same hollow, distant voice, "I feel so sad. Sad for the human race, for those who suffer, who are the victims of other people and don't even realize it, and for those who do realize it too. I'm sad for their executioners. Sad for the kind of men they are. Sad for humanity."

Mme. Weiser had disappeared.

*

. . .the name everyone wishes to pin on you, the one everyone is familiar with, the name that you needn't defend against intruders, against their indiscretion, but which you're supposed to be proud of, even show off. A name that does not differentiate you from any given object, a broom, a shoe, a cage — or whatever!

No, not that one. It's not necessary to either dissimulate or justify the legitimacy of that one. I mean the other one, the name you use when you happen to talk to yourself, the name that even your mother and father don't know, the one that was stamped into you before your birth. The name that is meant to set you free, set you free from the other one, set you free from everything. The name that anchors you in truth, and the one you would rather swallow your tongue than say out loud, give away. For, this is the name you'll give the Angel upon your . . . when one fine morning he sets the air around you ablaze . . .

*

Mme. Weiser had already placed her hand on the doorknob and was about to enter her son's room when she noticed a large white envelope at her feet. Intrigued, she bent down and picked it up. A letter. It had been slipped under the door from inside. Mme. Weiser read: "To Madame Myriam Weiser, David's Mother." She immediately recognized the handwriting — it was her son's. Mme. Weiser weighed the object thoughtfully in her hand.

Then, deciding not to go in, she turned and retraced her steps.

Holding the letter, she settled down in her favorite armchair in the living room. The envelope wasn't sealed, it was simply a matter of pulling out the flap that had been slipped inside. Her fingers were trembling now. Automatically, she reached for the eyeglasses, waiting to be used, on a nearby table. She began to read. And the air — though she hadn't read very far at all — the air seemed so scarce. She raised her free hand as if to touch her throat, tried to breathe; the hand only traveled halfway to her breast, then it fell to her lap.

Exodus

"So, you heard about it too. Can you believe it? They've really got the nerve, haven't they? What do you think, Gilbert?"

"Now what? Another bit of hot news that you're the only one to know anything about? Jesus Christ, Marcel! You've got a real knack for it. All right, out with it! What's the story today? Lord, I don't know where you dig them all up, but you're never at a loss."

"You ask me what the story is? Then you haven't even heard! Now that beats all! They've all cleared out. Every last one of them! Flown the coop! There's not a single one left."

"All of who?"

"I hit the nail right on the head, didn't I, eh?"

"No telling, come on, speak up first."

My table was near the bar where the two men were standing. One of them, the one named Marcel, was leaning on the counter with his elbows, glaring at the other, who simply stood there looking at his glass. Since the latter was nearest me and standing up to boot, I couldn't make out his features very well: little matter, I hadn't come there to study physiognomy. Or to listen to their stories either, for that matter.

Anyway, probably because the café was usually so noisy, the Marcel fellow–just him, not his buddy–was bellowing so hard you would have needed ear plugs to keep from hearing what he was talking about. It was pretty incredible stuff, judging from how excited he was getting.

It was pretty incredible, all right. Now that I know and am back here at my place thinking about it all again, I wish I'd been anywhere else but in that café at that particular time. I'd left one table, my work table, to go and sit down at another, a bar table, for a change of air. And then I run into to these two completely tactless guys, who aren't even aware that they're like two actors playing off each other's cues, and what do I hear?

"Yeah, pal, it doesn't really matter whether you believe it or not." (The Marcel fellow was going on like that.) "They're gone! Every last one of them! As if they'd been of one mind! We were snoozing, and they took a powder, in the middle of the night so no one would see them. Along with their bitches and their brats. All together, just like they were all part of one huge body."

The other fellow, Gilbert he was called, turned to face him now.

"Listen here, man, whenever you decide to stop talking in riddles, I might be able to catch what you're trying to say."

"I'm not kidding, what got into them?"

"Come on, Marcel, explain yourself. You keep raising hell about it, but you still haven't explained anything. What are you talking about? Who left?"

"No, it just can't be true. They must've all gone nuts."

I was listening in on this conversation, I just couldn't help it. All morning long I had sweated over five lines of text, only to sink deeper into an inextricable mire of crossed out, overworked, revised phrases with each new draft. Some days just aren't our day, nothing works. We can be perfectly aware of it but keep at it all the same, and it just gets us nowhere at all. Try as I might, in spite of obstinately starting over and over again as if my life depended on it, the whole fiasco ended as it should have long before: overwhelmed with the enormity of the task, I finally scrapped the damned lines. After that, air–some fresh air–I needed some air.

I had come down to the corner café. In my opinion, there's nothing like getting out and seeing people, watching them lead their lives, for setting one's mind straight. Then I had run into these two cards.

"The dark skins."

"The dark skins?"

"The wogs, the spades, those maguerrebin hustlers for you!

Suddenly, I was all ears. I didn't want to miss a word!

"Are you sure?"

"Sure? Damn right, I am!"

"You said all of them? Are you touched in the head or something?"

"It sure took a while, but you finally caught on. Every single one of them!"

"There must be a few of them left."

In suggesting this possibility, Gilbert's rugged, mercenary profile remained absolutely serious. However, judging from the tone of his voice, I would have sworn he was laughing inwardly.

"Zilch, zero Arabs, not a single one left not even down in those ratholes where they nested. So what do you have to say to that, eh?"

I was, and I always will be, one of those "maguerrebins" that this jerk was saying Lord knows what about: that they'd supposedly left the country, that they'd all packed their bags, every last one of them. He didn't seem to be joking either–on the contrary, he was dead serious. He also seemed to know perfectly well what he was talking about. No, how in God's name could something like that be possible? Every last one of them. And here I was sitting calmly in my neighborhood café!

Not feeling inclined to be any more tactful than they were, I listened to the rest of the story, paying particular attention to the figures of speech used, which seemed to be taken straight from the local folklore.

The other fellow, the one that was closest to me and whose profile was all I could make out, Gilbert, as he was called, then asked: "What're we going to do now?"

"What do you mean? What're we going to do now?" exclaimed Marcel. He had a bad habit of repeating what the person he was talking to had just said, but this time he had wanted to change the tone of the question.

"It's going to seem awful empty. Maybe some of them weren't really all that bad."

"Empty! I say we'll have a little breathing room, at last!"

A smile lit Marcel's bulging, beady eyes and somehow made that already well-rounded mug of his seem even plumper.

"Yeah, as a matter of fact, we'll breathe a lot easier now!"

"In my opinion, it's going to seem kind of empty," Gilbert repeated in the quiet voice that suited him so well.

"What's wrong, friend, you getting all worked up over a few wogs? A few good-for-nothings?"

"All I said was that it was going to seem empty."

"So what! We got rid of them without even having to dirty our hands! Believe it or not, you just happen to be looking at a man who had a good deal of ammo stashed away. You know, in case there was something that needed taking care of, something that just had to get done? In a way, it's a bit of a shame! But don't worry, the stash is still there. It just might come in handy some day. But it is a bit of a shame all the same."

Then Gilbert, ribbing him, adds: "A bit of a shame if it doesn't all turn out to be a lot of malarkey."

"Me, spread a lot of malarkey around? I heard about it on the radio, damn right I did!"

"And I say that both the radio and the television are full of malarkey."

"Meanwhile, I still got my stash of ammo and I don't plan on getting rid of it. So the Arabs turned tail? I say to hell with them all! We still got the others. There's a bunch of others. Now don't you start thinking they're all that counts anymore either. Like what's-his-face said, the world isn't full of nice, pretty people."

"Don't you think you're pushing things a bit far, Marcel? You're getting all worked up. You'll end up having a stroke if you don't watch out."

"Dear comrade and registered member of the union, take my word for it–don't ever let them get the upper hand. If I was told tomorrow that there was a war going on right out there in the street, I'd answer: 'count me in.' I'm not one for laissez faire or the English wet-and-sea."

"Never heard of it."

"At any rate that's what they say on the other side of the Channel."

"What channel?"

"That little strip of ocean up north."

Immediately after he provided this explanation, something strange happened–Marcel grew suddenly pensive, his whole pudgy face and body seemed to be laboring over something. He stood there for a moment in complete silence, which was obviously something he was not accustomed to.

Finally, he came to a decision and declared with a frown, "It's definitely a shame, all right. At least they could have left a few behind."

Gilbert, looking perplexed, didn't seem to know what to make of this statement. Standing there quite tall and strong, rough-boned, his profile seemed to be chiseled out of stone. Behind that deeply furrowed brow, he must have been seriously mulling it all over.

As for me, I had thoroughly understood.

I had understood precisely because I was one of the immigrants that had all supposedly emigrated in the opposite direction. Every single one of them, with the exception of myself. Having missed the signal to depart, I was probably the only one left. There was nothing mysterious about the fact that I had been completely in the dark about it all. In this neighborhood, you never run into so much as the shadow of one of my compatriots, so if word had gone around, it had simply never reached me.

Also, even if those two jokers had noticed me, they would never have dreamed that I was one of those "maguerrebins" they were so up in arms about, or even if they did know that one of them had been left behind, they'd never guess that I was the culprit. Nature had endowed me with a physical appearance that made it easy for me to melt into the sea of the general population. As a matter of fact, it suddenly occurred to me that I'd been a citizen of this country before being considered a foreigner.

"Even if those young punks, those teenage brats, those skinheads, are all that's left, now that the wogs are out of the picture, you'll still have your hands plenty full," jeered Gilbert. "Isn't that right, Marcel?"

"Shit! Why in the hell did they up and leave? What'd they have against us? I just don't get it. Our country wasn't good enough for them? They'll have nothing but dirt to eat back where they come from, I can tell you that much. The bastards! I had a few of them right next door to me. I got along just fine with them. Think I should've told them to stay?"

The fellow named Gilbert just kept harping on the same old string, "It's gonna seem awful empty, that's for sure."

Judging from his knotty profile, it was easy to see that he wasn't the talkative type and, above all, that the whole matter didn't really interest him. He was taking part in the conversation simply to please the other man.

"You're damned right it will!" Marcel exclaimed indignantly pounding his fist down on the metal counter. "What in the hell got into them? Since they were already here, why didn't they just stay on! No really, who do they think they are anyway? Did they expect us to get down on our knees and beg them to stay or something?"

With a tray balanced on one hand, the waiter passed by within earshot. I signaled him to come over. "Could you please tell me what day this is?"

He seemed completely taken aback. However, I noticed that he too thought about it before answering me, as if he were obviously addressing someone who wasn't quite all there.

"Yes of course, sir, today is Friday. Friday, April 29. Would you like to know what year it is too?"

Concentrating on trying to etch that date indelibly into my memory, I said absentmindedly, "I see. . . . Are you sure?"

He was beginning to get an offended look on his face but changed his mind and walked away shaking his head.

Now what am I to do? I am the one who has to answer that question. Because I couldn't see past the tip of my own pen, I've gone and missed the boat again. I had gotten into the habit of using my pen as an instrument of divination. I have so much fun at practicing the geomancy that writing is compared to, through which I thought I could foretell the meanderings of my own life and even those of the world. But the oracle does not always pronounce himself, and this time he had remained silent. My countrymen had kept me company, albeit from afar. I could decide to go and join them whenever I felt like it, even though the desire rarely manifested itself. Now they are gone, and here I am alone, left with my tablet of sand upon which I can trace sign after sign, ad infinitum, and still remain utterly alone. And I can imagine the sort of welcome they will get, how everyone has prepared for the event back home. What a celebration there will be. What excitement. I put myself in the place of those awaiting their return, crowded around the airfields, on the docks in the ports, in the train stations. I can hear the hurrahs that will rise from all the throats as if in a single cry. Honoring their brothers and sisters who have come home from exile, their thundering acclamations seem to shake the very depths of heaven and earth.

I can see them weeping with joy.

A Game of Dice

They had shown them the door. Two boys — one eighteen, the other, maybe twenty. Eighteen and twenty years old, no more. They had said to them, "There it is." They had said to them, "It's never locked." It was closed. They pushed it. It opened. They went in. Or rather they burst into the courtyard, a large patio. It would be light for quite some time yet — the curfew would sound, and it would still be light. Here it was lighter than day — one couldn't tell why — lighter than it was out in the city. And that silence. It was impossible explain what it was like. The patio was shimmering with muteness and solitude. They had said to them, "He lives alone."

They had said to them, "With this man, there'll be no problem. You just go there. He lives alone. An old man. And everything will go smoothly."

They had said to them, "It'll be a piece of cake."

And in that silence, like an amplified gasp, incongruous, a shot cracked out. A gasp, and it hit one of the two boys, who, seized with a sort of convulsion, fell. One bullet, a single shot. He fell and didn't move again. The other swung around, ran toward the door that he hadn't realized coming through would provoke an out-break of deadly wasps. A door, that door. They had simply said to them, "No, it's never locked." He knew it now. He was pulling it, pulling on it, but it wasn't opening, and there were these wasps, these bullets. He was pulling with all his might, and nothing. It wasn't opening. They had said to them, "It's never locked."

"Don't waste your strength, son. It's operated electrically. Come a little closer."

A calm, mature voice. Paternal. One that almost no one had ever used with him before. It was that kind of voice, and it was inviting him to come over rather than ordering him to do so.

He turned around.

"Do come closer, my boy."

He remained with his back pinned up against the door, the door he now understood the workings of. The voice still sounded amiable, engaging. It was perfect for making someone feel at ease.

Old, this man? He must not be that old. He was speaking from one of the rooms, apparently from the room directly opposite the door. His face, if he even had a face, if he wasn't just the voice by itself, still couldn't be distinguished. No, he must not be that old. And the other boy, lying in the same spot where he'd crumpled up, wasn't moving. A target hit, on the very first shot. Definitely hit. Not so bad for an old man. He must not be that old.

"I told you to come forward."

The boy took three steps, then one more step.

The man fired.

The boy squawked like a hoarse rooster, "For God's sake!"

He had come here to kill, not to die. He hadn't wanted this. He dropped to his knees.

The man continued to fire. The boy, kneeling, was praying.

"Lord God. . . . Lord God . . ."

Then it was tears — fear sweating, a prayer rising from deep in the entrails, welling up into the eyes — that spoke as they streamed down over his face. It wasn't fair to die so young.

A shot. A pause. A shot. A pause.

None of them hit him. None of them tore through his skin anywhere, blinded him. "I would have felt it," he thought.

But how can you be sure? God, how? If one of them makes your head explode, are you aware of it? Another one came. The gunman was not one to miss a target. Still another shot. The bullets grazed past him, whistled as they went skimming by his ears. He was waiting for the one that would end it all, snuff out the daylight. The curfew would sound.

They stopped coming. The man was calling out to him, "How are you doing?"

What could he answer to his *how are you doing?*

"Well, son?"

The boy understood: the man was torturing him first — afterwards, he would kill him. He could have brought him down with the first shot if he had wanted to, like the other boy, slumped over there only a few feet away. With the very first shot.

A tremendous silence flooded over the patio. The man was reloading his gun, obviously. The maneuver finished with a click, and that was all: the silence that had momentarily receded filled the patio again.

The man was not firing.

Crouching down, the boy was contemplating the uniformly red tile floor that faded out to light brown around the edges of the courtyard — undoubtedly because of the coming twilight, but also, he was sure, to imitate the other boy's blood. His companion lying over there in the puddle of red blood that had oozed out and was turning brown as it dried.

He counted the tiles. He counted the vanishing cracks between the tiles. He wondered if he had ever counted anything from this close up or from this far away before. The last thing he would ever see but the first thing he would see as no one else had ever seen it, and it was something totally inconsequential. He contemplated it: everything was going to stop right here, his life would be over.

Yes, you remember that boy. He was alive and now he's dead, That's all he ever did. Just play, and now he's dead. He got involved in the terrorist movement for the fun of it, and he's gone now. So young. Maybe he didn't even realize it when it happened.

He was waiting. To know that you will soon be leaving this world and know exactly when you will learn it, exactly when this unprecedented knowledge will be bestowed upon you. Not moving, and the only thing that even enters your mind is the knowledge, which won't be of much use to you.

"Have you ever killed anyone, son?"

"No, sir."

"But you came here with your companion to kill me?"

"Yes, sir."

"What wrong have I done?"

"To man, none."

"So, why?"

"You have wronged God."

"Was it God who told you that?"

"Not to me, sir."

"To whom then!"

"To the chief."

"So God confides in the chief."

"I don't know, sir."

"Do you talk with him yourself?"

"With God?"

"With the chief."

"No, sir."

"And with God?"

The boy, still kneeling, cowered down even lower, did not answer that.

Bizarre, the silence that had fallen between them, in which they took refuge: far from separating them, it opened out onto another language, conveyed the violent call of blood that could not find the right words, at least not yet.

Then the man said, "And God told him that I must be killed."

"Yes, sir."

By way of an answer, it had been more of a gurgling that had come not from the boy's throat but from far away, from over the distance of incertitude, of fear, of unsolved questions.

"Did God tell him," the man continued, "that you would die too?"

"No, I don't believe he told him anything like that."

"What a child! In any case, you are going to die. Look at your companion, the cadaver that he's become, that you too will become. Look at him, I say."

The boy turned a tortured face toward the other boy, the cadaver now.

"Do you think that it is fair or not?"

"That what is fair or not, sir?"

"That you should be killed as well."

"I don't know what to reply, sir."

"But they, the ones who sent you, they've already got their answer: for them, it doesn't matter whether you die or not. You knew that before you came."

"Yes, sir."

"No, you didn't know it! You're lying! Just like all of your friends, you thought you'd find yourself confronted with a stupid, defenseless fool. Someone that can be killed without running the slightest risk. Not the slightest risk. Go on, tell me, isn't that true?"

"Yes, sir, it's true."

"Meanwhile, the same loving voice was silently digging it's way under the words. It was digging, and it was bleeding.

"Is this your first time, son?"

"Yes, sir."

"Did you know whom you had come to kill?"

"No, sir."

"But the ones who sent you, they knew. For them it wouldn't have been an easy task, for they knew who they were dealing with. Now you know as well as they do that you were being sent to your death."

"I'll just ...," began the boy. He heaved a sigh, like a child before tears come.

"You'll just what?" the man insisted.

"I'll just have to die. I don't expect life or anyone else to ..."

The boy had stopped there. And the man, in a very strange tone of voice given the circumstances, said, "So you believe, regarding your deceased comrade, that he is happier than you?"

The boy remained silent.

"I'm asking you, Do you believe your comrade to be happier dead than alive?"

"Yes, sir!" answered the boy in a voice loud enough to break the windows had the house happened to have any but that only shattered the silence, the luminous void that enveloped the patio.

"Do you now know what one goes through when faced with death?" the man cried back almost as loudly.

In the same tone of voice the boy assented, "Yes, sir!"

"Then you know what your victim goes through the instant he sees you put the knife to his throat."

"Yes, sir."

"And what if his soul came back to ask you to justify your act while you were sleeping, what would you answer?"

The boy didn't need to think about it much. He replied immediately, "That in losing your life in a shit-hole of a country, you don't lose all that much."

"Let's keep it polite, son. Now, throw down your arm."

Obediently, the poor child reached his hand into his breast pocket, drew out a cutlass, and held it up.

"Put it on the floor," the man ordered from his position in one of the windows, without showing himself.

"Is that all?"

"I swear to it."

Only then did the man appear. He walked over and kicked the knife away, out into the center of the courtyard. Standing over him, he then put the barrel of his pistol to the top of the boy's head.

Again, the kneeling hero let out that awful squawking sound of a hoarse rooster.

"For the love of God, don't do it, sir. Don't kill me. Treat me as a father would his son."

And his prayers turned to sobs.

"As a father."

He was sobbing, sniffling while the man cursorily and expertly searched him and discovered no other arms.

"Get up."

The boy stumbled to his feet. In the same imperious voice, the man asked him, "What's your name?"

"Azzedine, sir."

"And you, Azzedine, would you have spared my life had I been in your place?"

The boy kept his lips pinched tightly together, but his eyes were opened so wide and they were so clear it would have been impossible to get them to focus on you.

Up until now, he had not actually seen the man but only heard his voice coming from one of the rooms. Seeing him now, the boy realized that he towered over him by at least a head.

"Unfortunately, your attempt failed, and now you're at my mercy. Do you understand that?"

The man was butting the end of his pistol up against the boy's chest as he spoke.

"You never imagined when you busted in here that you'd be risking your life and maybe . . . even lose it. You and your kind — tempting the devil, or shall we say tempting Providence, isn't exactly your cup of tea, is it? You won't commit murder unless you're insured against all risks."

The boy's eyes were completely vacant. He responded neither yes or no, didn't move.

"Now your life is mine to do with as I will. Have we got that straight now?"

The boy cast those same eyes, devoured with wild light, up at the person standing over him, at the emaciated body dressed in a very ordinary gray suit, the sinewy body, and face too, sinewy, tanned, tough, a cutthroat. And yet a cutthroat who under that thick hide was not devoid of feelings, despite the hatchet-nose, despite the swollen, blood-red mouth, and, above all, those eyes, sharp as ice picks, which seemed to complete the picture perfectly.

"We've got it straight all right. What are you waiting for?" said the boy.

"I'm waiting for you to stop that goggling before you die."

The adolescent didn't seem to hear these words any more than he seemed to be able to see the man standing in front of him. And yet the sleepwalker, whose life was in his hands, couldn't keep his lips from trembling either.

"Don't be in such a hurry, son. There's no such thing as losing time when it comes to dying. You can only gain time. I've decided to offer you a second chance. Your wretched life — which is mine, right? — I'll play a game of dice with you for it. Sit down."

The boy, who seemed completely confused, did not obey immediately, not knowing whether to submit himself to such preposterous nonsense. What should he do?

"Sit down, I said," the man repeated. "This time you will be fully informed of what the stakes are when you put your life on the line: either you win and you'll leave here alive, as you came in, or else you lose . . . you lose . . . and I'd like to believe that you'll show as much courage as you did when you came to murder an ostensibly defenseless person."

The boy suddenly resembled someone who was awakening from a long sleep. As he had resolved to do from the time he realized he was defeated, he confined his answers to repeating, in a somber, laconic voice, "Yes, sir."

Rapidly, mechanically, he dropped back down to his knees and waited. The man agilely squatted down to face him and even crossed his legs as a fakir might. He had already slipped his free hand into his pocket while he continued to aim his gun at the boy. He quickly pulled out two dice, which he set down side by side on the tile floor.

With the same skittish reserve, the boy asked, "How is the game played?"

"It's very simple."

Rolling the dice over on each of their sides, the man explained succinctly the rules of the game.

*

Thrown by the man, the dice rolled, spun with a giddy sound like a watchman's rattle, and then, thrown by the boy also, they rolled, spun — party crackers popping whose bounding and bouncing the boy followed with awestruck eyes. Spellbound, forgetting every-thing — the patio, what he had come here to do, the circumstances which had led him to this place — the boy shot the dice. The man shot the dice, then they both shot again, their gestures regulated as if by an irremediably mindless metronome. They didn't exchange a word except, having seen from the very first game the minimal ef-fect his explanations had, the man took it upon himself to inform the boy of the scores. Of his — the boy's — scores, and of his — the man's — scores. He was like a strange talking machine, answering itself of its own accord.

Still, luck did not favor either of them. Each new roll of the dice negated the adversary's. As a matter of fact, although the boy could hear his score being announced, it didn't seem to sink in or make any difference to him at all. The rules of the game eluded him, his life eluded him, as did everything else — and he just kept on throwing those dice. The voice, which he couldn't listen to but which he couldn't help hearing, droned on as well, gnawing at his ear, clear, concise, monotonous.

Apparently for the sake of fairness — and why not of pedagogy too — the man said again: "With a two you win two points, a three will get you three, a four also four, and a five, five. But the double six you just rolled — like mine, did you notice? — that gets you sixty points twice over! We're back at zero to zero again. One thing es-capes me: how can people who commit murder, and often in the most ruthless manner, pretend to be acting in the interest of their fellow men — and doing God's will to boot — even though their victims have done nothing wrong and can't even be accused of being impious? Could you please explain that to me?"

Hypnotized by the wild dancing of the dice, the boy did not answer, or thought he didn't need to answer.

"Very well," said the man. "Why should you explain these things? You just carry out orders, and it's up to the chiefs to give reasons. However, you won't be spared hearing about what you people did to a young mother last Wednesday night. Right in front of her daughters, you slit her throat, even though she had just begged you to have the mercy of killing her somewhere else. Then you tore her head off, which you threw out into the street. After performing this great feat of heroism, you turned tail and ran, and the oldest child had to go and find her mother's head to put it back on the body."

The man stopped playing just long enough to ask a question: "What do you have to say about that?"

Suddenly sounds came rushing through the boy's lips, his reply gushing out in a torrent of words: "Life should be held accountable for it all! With all the hardships it puts us through, it is life that should pay for its wrongs, not us! Life pushes us around, shamelessly trampling everyone underfoot! Only death can bring pardon. Pardon, mercy . . ."

The voice, fading into a desperate flatness, wasn't addressing the man. It wasn't addressing anyone.

"It's life that spreads terror and horror everywhere — that's its way of watching over us. Death just follows along behind, picking up the pieces."

The man let him speak.

Soon, the boy was having trouble spitting out the scraps of sentences that were stuck in his throat — nothing but rattling sounds were coming from his mouth.

"Life betrayed us. . . . And you . . . you . . . a- a- . . . adults . . . , you, the men who . . . who came before us — you too have . . . have betrayed the confidence that . . . we put in you!"

"So, now we're playing the game of truth," the man replied. "You've finally come to realize that, son."

Although he seemed to be far from running out of arguments, the man said no more. There were a million things he could have added, but his philosophy was obviously to never reveal his most intimate thoughts to just anyone.

What was it, then, that in the very next second inexplicably spurred him to go on? He must have had a reason for deciding to do so.

"This game was first begun long ago, son. It was begun before you set foot in this house, before you started brandishing your knife at your own people, even before you were born. Before everything. It's your turn to play now. What are you waiting for? We believe we can change the course of events and, in so doing, the course of our destiny. Never. Impossible. We only delay their coming to fruition, and the longer they are postponed the more forcefully they come back, all the more efficiently destructive. And as for our destiny, it smirks as it watches us gesticulating in vain."

And in turn, he let out a laugh that wasn't really a laugh, a laugh that crackled like a match that goes out as soon as you strike it.

Then he added, "But we just can't abstain from playing at pitting ourselves against destiny. Playing in the same way that you're playing for your life right now. That's just the way things are."

He also made this strange remark: "Even so, we learn to know ourselves. You know who you are now."

"No, not yet."

"A murderer."

"No, not yet."

"Oh, yes."

"No, I'm not a murderer. I'm nobody. And you, master, can't be teaching me who I am because, unfortunately for you, it's too late to teach me anything. You've missed the boat."

"Oh yes. I've already taught you things, and you know perfectly well that I'm still teaching you things — how to distinguish one thing from another, how to open your eyes and acknowledge what you are and know you'll have to pay for it."

"You haven't even taught me what I should call myself and you haven't even deigned to use my name, Azzedine, since you asked me what it was. And if you haven't, I suppose it's because you don't know what to call yourself either and because you too are a nobody, just as I am!"

"What about drugs?" the man asked.

"They bring me closer to God, to myself, to my country, to everything we have lost, to what I have lost."

"And murder, does it also bring you closer to all of this?"

"Yes, murder too."

"How can you affirm such a thing? Until now, you have never committed one if you were telling the truth before. It's an experience you've never had, and don't you realize that the murder, which you're now in a difficult position to commit, would kill you too? Wouldn't that matter to you?"

Then it was the young terrorist's turn to burst out in bitter, mocking laughter.

"Matter? That committing a crime would kill me? But there's nothing left in me to kill! I'm nothing but pain as far down as you can reach. I'm nothing but an open, festering wound. I'm nothing but a dead man suffering from not being all the way dead yet. Can you understand that?"

The man pointed out, "You just took your turn, didn't you? Then pass me the dice, please."

And there was nothing more between them but the sound of the dice rattling, skipping over the bare tile floor and the silence — a complete silence that enveloped them and seemed to bear down upon the walls of the square patio, pushing them out towards a horizon that had a distinctly twilight, ghost-like appearance. It was the time of day, however, when night had just barely dispatched its shadows — shadows that only slipped, insinuated their translucent tentacles in between the two players in refusing to change anything around them, a man and a boy who, in any case, were paying absolutely no attention to the shade of amber the light had taken on or to the fact that nothing had changed around them.

With his eyes glued to the dice as they raced across the floor, the man went on, "Are you familiar with these words from the Book? 'Verily, if you lift your hand to kill me, I will not lift my hand to kill you.' Surah five, verse twenty-eight. What do you think of that?"

The boy shook his head in refusal several times before answering.

"Don't waste your time — I'm not familiar with it. If I could have killed you, I would have."

"'Be responsible for your crime against me, bear my sin and your own, and be counted amongst the hosts of Fire.'"

Having again recited rather than simply spoken these words, the man declared in his normal voice, "Same surah, verse twenty-nine."

"What of it! What is a human life in God's eyes, can you tell me that?"

The man said jokingly, "Nothing. Outside of your own, of course."

"Outside of my own? Not at all."

"Then with the exception of your chief's?"

"I have no idea."

"You're lying again. No idea? Your head is full of them, and you can see where they've gotten you. You do see, don't you?"

"I don't see."

"And who does see? No one? God?"

"God sees."

"And who else? Your chief?"

"I don't know."

"God will tell him."

"Maybe."

"And afterwards, you'll go on just exactly as you always have."

"Not me, but the others, yes, in the name of God. As for me, when I look at you, all I can see is death staring me in the face. That's all I have to look forward to."

"Silly child! Have you any idea why we kill a sheep to celebrate l'Aïd Kébir?"

"No, sir."

"Abraham wanted to sacrifice his son Ishaq in God's name, and God refused the offering. Instead, in the place of the child, God put a sheep under Abraham's knife. That's why. So that he, who professed to be human, should not kill another human being. Who was Abraham, do you have any idea?"

"No, sir."

"And does your chief know?"

"I don't know about him, sir."

Dusk came, not drifting in from the sky in successive waves but creeping in little by little from the walls, the outer edges of the patio already more than half dissolved in a dim haze and stopped, sparing the players, at the rim of the impregnable circle of light they were sitting in the center of.

It had never occurred to the man to scrutinize the young terrorist so closely before. Above all, he had probably wanted to avoid doing so, avoid having to confront the feelings that the pale face outlined with the dark beginnings of a beard would inspire in him. What words could describe the milky, inexpressive face, wide at the top but tapering down to a dimpled, jutting chin? Or those lips unfolding like the wings of a bird and, over them, the short nose with a finely grooved tip, the forehead running flat down to the eyes — eyes that were terrifyingly transparent? The man clenched his teeth. Death hiding behind the mask of an adolescent. It had

those wide-open eyes gaping out into, one couldn't tell, some unknown distance — a watchful and recurring illusion.

"You won, son. Get out now. Leave right away. Do you hear me,
Azzedine? You can leave, I say. Alive, whole, just as you came."

Those eyes, he couldn't tear his from them.

"Essentially, you — all of you, you and your kind — are nothing
but our own personal demons. We've always carried you deep
within ourselves. And because we weren't skillful or clever enough
to keep you chained up where you should have been, here you are,
free to move about, free to infest the earth and, like howling
wolves, forever call up the past."

As soon as he heard these words, the boy was on his feet and,
without a word, turned his back to the man.

He was already at the door when an order, one last order,
stopped him in his tracks.

"Hold on there, stop! Wait till I open the door for you! And your
cumbersome partner there, you won't forget to take him along,
will you?"

The boy waited. He didn't wonder what he should do — he had
no choice.

The man went into one of the rooms, which only took him a few
seconds, and came back to join him. He personally took him by the
arm and led him over to the dead man, who was almost lying across
the doorstep. He helped him hoist the cadaver onto one shoulder.
Having accomplished that task, the boy was getting ready to open
the door when, with a click, he saw it swing open by itself.

He went out. The night lay heavily upon the city. Then he was
gone. The man followed him with his eyes, sent him this blessing:
"Good riddance, son."

The curfew had emptied the streets. Staggering, doubled over
under the weight of the lifeless body, the boy set out breathing
wildly and with a sudden urge to vomit in his stomach. He
wouldn't let himself go, he fought it. But he just couldn't resist,

he let go. Nothing came. And then it came. But it wasn't what he'd thought — it was wrenching sobs that he was vomiting up.

Sobs? Why? Did he regret not having been killed too? Because now he'll have no pity on the world, he . . .

It began, far behind him, dull thuds that at first he merely sensed without really being conscious of them. And the noise was advancing, getting closer, a black noise, something like the rushing sound that the wings of a thousand vampires would make. Over that sound, shots started ringing out. "Shots that the old man is firing? Are they catching up with me?" Although he felt like it, he refrained from running, he simply took quicker steps. "In the end they'll . . . ," he tripped, stumbled, carried along under the weight of his dead burden. "In the end they'll . . . ," he thought.

Afterword

If, by reason of their underlying similarities, we consider the body of an author's novels collectively as a different, larger novel, encompassing all the others, should not his short stories also be viewed as the component parts of a novel that, consisting of various offshoots from a single tree and linked by the same underlying similarities, will, in its turn, add to the master-novel? All things considered, this is a point of view that one could adopt in reading the short stories in this collection, although each of them can stand entirely on its own and warrants being read individually.

One of the main things that ties these stories together is an implicit question: How can we, in our shared humanity, have allowed ourselves to be a party to the great wrongs of this century and, in so doing, create an era of even more prolific crimes? It would be asking too much to attempt to answer the *why* of this question; the least we can do is state the *how*, expose human beings for the insidious buffoons they are, engaged in the insidious farces of this insidious time. Can the mere fact that we have set foot on the moon excuse or redeem humanity? Nothing could be more uncertain. What if it were simply in preparation for other crimes?

We can still call upon the children, our children, to be our witnesses. They are the protagonists of several of these short stories. What hope can we place in them if we mold them in our own image?

However, it is not a writer's job to mete out lessons but to reverse the learning process. He does not prescribe responses but rather poses questions.

Another character in these short stories is the Hunter. Invisible, yet nevertheless omnipresent, he represents violence that is indifferent, unlimited, devoid of all feeling. He could be considered the incarnation of the Devil if he were a sly, rapacious tempter. Yet he is none of these things.

The one concern that I have never been able to address without breaking out in anxious beads of sweat is the idea of continuity in a story, the thing that by some miracle, or some curse, structures it, brings to life that which was initially but a disparate conglomerate, a galaxy of miniature narratives. Where might we unearth the secret of this alchemy, and how can it be captured and mastered? Can the thing that runs through a narrative, giving one the feeling that time and life have been infinitely expanded and providing a deep sense of satisfaction, be found within the narrative itself? Or, upon closer examination, does it actually lie within ourselves? Is it something we developed when we first began to read, and from that moment onward our reading became the result of an ongoing synthesis of elements that are, in reality, fundamentally unrelated? Might it not reside in our ability to reincarnate into each and every character? Perhaps continuity simply stems from the dynamics of writing itself. Unless it originates in something even farther removed, a sort of destiny, one might say, is the driving force of fiction just as it determines the path of humanity and dictates down to the very unfolding of a tale — a tale as fictitious as one could expect the true story of our lives to be if it were related by a voluble sphinx.

It is difficult to understand how continuity functions simply because we are its prisoners, I believe. Dreamers, absorbed in their dreams, are not surprised by breaks, discrepancies, *solutions of continuity* that they encounter throughout the dream-tale; they are only aware of the underlying coherence of incidents, which alone hold meaning for them. Whether in the process of writing or reading, we also live in a dream world. And we emerge from a novel that we are writing or reading as we emerge from a dream: with only one question in our minds, *what imparts meaning?* In my opinion, it can only be the mystery that eternally shrouds the phenomenon of continuity and that I find myself forever cursing.

And what if it were like an inn in which guests were served only that which they brought along with them? But let us not dwell upon this aspect of the problem.

What could be of more importance for a writer than to be confronted with the issue of one's own responsibility? The question is not aptly put, it should be reversed. It would be more appropriate to ask, Is there any point in churning out reams of written pages if one is not held accountable for it? Accountable for having written it all or for simply having written at all. The Western world seems to have extricated itself from this problem by separating the two things: writing (fiction) and responsibility (morals). Should we, can we, uphold this point of view under any and all circumstances? I don't think that we can or that we should. It doesn't even matter what I think, it becomes increasingly obvious every day. Yet all that is so far from the Western world.

*

It is not my wish to see writers close ourselves up in the role of lesson-givers or censors, but on the other hand, we should deem it only natural to run into sanctions when we state (write) what we believe "in our heart of hearts." What better way of learning the value of the written word or discovering that one's words have impact, that they gain in value in direct proportion to the blame incurred or the extent of the condemnation they inspire? The fact that writing entails a risk restores a certain stamp of nobility to literature. Yet today, it is less a question of nobility than one of simple survival in the vast and chattering desert that has spread over a large part of the planet.

Of course, in the midst of this cacophony, the writer can still hold out hope, and nurture the sense of gratification born of this hope, that one day, an unknown reader will hear his or her words.

And I would certainly not go so far as to condemn a society in the name of glorifying literature (or denouncing its turpitude).